Always A Grunt

I0641439

MIKE LEDINGHAM

BMS Books
5 High Street
Rotorua, 3010
New Zealand

Published in June 2014 by BMS Books
An imprint of Business Media Services Limited
5 High Street, Rotorua 3010
P.O. Box 6215, Whakarewarewa
Rotorua 3010, New Zealand
Tel: 64-7-349 4107
Email: ms@bms.co.nz
Web site: www.bms.co.nz
All rights reserved.

ISBN: 978-0-473-29049-8

Published in Kindle
ISBN: 978-0-473-29050-4

Published in E-pub
ISBN: 978-0-473-29051-1

ABOUT THE AUTHOR

Mike Ledingham, who lives in Featherston, Wairarapa, has enjoyed a colourful career as a farmhand, soldier, small businessman, real estate salesman, hospital orderly, armed security guard and more. Most of these offbeat stories are based loosely on events he has witnessed or been involved in.

Follow the *Once A Grunt* page on Facebook to keep up with news about Mike and his writing.

ABOUT *ALWAYS A GRUNT*

Readers of Mike Ledingham's first book, *Once a Grunt,* will be familiar with the characters in many of these stories. As with the first book, the characters in *Always a Grunt* are loosely categorized into military-related and non-military yarns. There are also a couple of uncategorized stories, both of them emotionally intense. They are Nessy's Story, which deals with raw grief, and The Boy, which describes a child's struggle with sexual abuse.

·

CONTENTS

INTRODUCTION

Once again, there is a vein of truth running through a lot of these stories, and once again, I have taken it further. So they are not true.

Having said that, there are a couple that are closer to the truth than one would ever really want them to be. But I'll leave it to the reader to figure out which ones they are.

Once again, I'm indebted to friends and family for ongoing encouragement and support, especially my brother Peter for the long hours spent in fixing up my erratic English. Thanks also to Mike Smith from BMS Books for his forbearance and patience.

One day, maybe, I'll get to Whitireia and do that creative writing course. Hopefully before I peg it.

Enjoy!

Mike Ledingham
Featherston, January 2014

NESSY

NESSY'S STORY

In loving memory of Vanessa Mary Lola Ledingham
10/9/89 - 24/7/92
Your star will always shine in our hearts, Nessy.
Moe moea.
And for anyone who has known the pain of losing a child.

The pup was the result of a mistake at a breeding kennel. The wrong dog had gotten into the wrong cage at the wrong time and of course the resulting crossbreeds weren't exactly welcomed with open arms.

There was talk of putting the pups down immediately but one of the staff was horrified at this prospect and promised to find them homes. Permission was reluctantly granted, but a time proviso was attached.

The German pointer/border collie cross pups were real cuties and once weaned the three males were quickly snapped up, leaving only the female. When the time proviso ran out, the staff member reluctantly took the female home – not exactly an ideal solution, given where she lived in the city.

Somehow, through a friend of a friend of a friend, a home was finally found for the pup. It was seven months old and a big floppy, ungainly, delirious bundle of joy and energy.

The couple had met in the army, she a Maori girl from down south and he a fourth-generation pakeha of Irish/Scottish ancestry. Once the children had started coming, she had taken her discharge from the army to become a mother. Because he was away a lot, and they lived in South Auckland, they both thought that it would be good to have a dog for security. And so the pup found a permanent home.

The pup loved the children and followed them everywhere, especially the boy. There were three of them by now, a boy and two girls. The boy was nearly four, the oldest girl was two and there was a newborn baby girl.

The father's brother was heading off to Australia and put on a barbecue for the rest of the family. Of course, the dog went as well. It was part of the family.

The brother lived next to a large reserve covered in bush and with a creek running through it. Somehow during the festivities, the boy managed to slip away, and when this was discovered, people were soon searching and calling fruitlessly, and beginning to get very worried.

"Hang on," said the brother. "Where's the dog? Call the dog!"

The father called and whistled out and was immediately answered by barking, from right down near the creek. They raced down, and there was the boy right beside the creek, with the dog in the water pointing at him, as if to say: "Don't come in here, you little bugger." The dog was the hero of the day but couldn't understand what all the fuss was about. She'd just looked after her family, hadn't she?

The father got sick of being away from home all the time, took his discharge from the army and the family moved even further north for his new job. Another child arrived, a boy. Then 18 months later another girl was born, very tiny and with two holes in her heart.

The prognosis was not good. "She probably won't last the year," said the doctor. "Take her home and love her while you've got her." The little girl was a happy, cheeky little thing who always had cold feet and hands and a tiny button of a bright red nose because her heart was not efficient.

Despite being sick often and spending some time in hospital, she proved the doctors wrong and celebrated her first birthday. She loved her Mum and Dad, brothers and sisters and especially the dog. She had the dog wrapped round her little finger. At night, from the time she could crawl and was out of the cot and into a bed, she would always crawl into her parents' bedroom, bat her father across the face calling "da-da" until he woke up and put her in the bed. She always had to be right between the two of them.

"It's all right for you," the mother complained to the father. "She always wants her head on your arm and her feet on me. She always kicks her socks off, and her feet are freezing." But then the Mum had to do the drugs and the nasty bits, while the Dad only did the cuddling and the sympathy.

When the other kids were at school or kohanga reo, the dog would always sneak into her bedroom and just lie with her head on her paws and watch the little girl sleep. If she woke up and put her hand out, the dog would lick her, and they'd play and laugh.

The child defied the doctors again and made her second birthday. But her tiny life was becoming ever more difficult to sustain. She struggled throughout the following summer, and the winter was especially hard for her. Any sort of illness usually meant a trip to hospital and at times she would turn blue because her heart was not efficient.

The parents were under strict instructions to call an ambulance whenever this occurred and not to take her to the hospital themselves. The waiting time always seemed forever, and it's hard for parents to sit by helplessly and watch their child struggle for life. The dog always hated it when the child was sick or away in hospital.

Time was obviously running out so the parents asked the doctors: "Could you not have a look to see if there is anything that can be done?"

An appointment was made with a specialist and eventually the Mum and Dad took their tiny, sick, brave little girl to Auckland for a do-or-die operation. The Mum was to stay at the hospital while the Dad headed back up north, so she bought the little girl out to see Dad off into the lift. They played peekaboo with the lift door for a while, and the little girl erupted into delighted gales of laughter. A final hug and a kiss and the Dad left.

It was after 9pm, the kids were in bed and the Dad was sitting at the table, the dog at his feet, wondering and hoping, when there was a knock at the door. It was the people over the road – husband, wife, two kids. They didn't have to say anything, from the look on their faces the Dad knew. "She hasn't made it, has she?" Tears were shed and then the Dad left for Auckland.

By the time they got back up north with their little girl the following day, their house had been turned into a mini marae. The wives from the rugby club and members of the kohanga reo had taken charge and cleaned and readied the house. The kids were all being looked after, two sisters were organizing the kitchen and Kenny, an old mate from up north, had turned up with his mother, gas cookers and bottles, thrown a tarp over the back deck and was cooking up huge amounts of food.

A local kaumatua had taken charge of the formal side of proceedings and the parents, after being called in and protocol observed, entered into discussion about where they were going to bury the baby – important, because the mother was not from a local iwi.

The kaumatua offered a plot at his family urupa out at the coast, but the parents politely declined, saying they wanted to bury her locally so they could visit often, take flowers and talk to her. This was accepted.

People began to arrive. Lots of people. People they knew. People they didn't know. They came because a child had died, and they wanted to stand with the family, share their grief and extend their aroha.

The kuia, Kenny's mum and old Rewa and Ruby, stayed there the whole time. Ruby sang her song. "Don't chase the sparrows away, don't chase the sparrows away, just give them some crumbs and they'll be your chums, you might be a sparrow someday."

More and more people and many strangers arrived. They came because a child had died.

Envelopes and gifts of food were passed on to the sisters while Kenny and the dog were still out on the deck. Him cooking and the dog ... well, the dog wasn't very happy. She wouldn't eat.

Two vanloads of people from the wife's iwi arrived in the wee small hours of the second day. Again, after the protocol had been observed, the discussion turned to where the child was going to be buried. The local kaumatua took up the parents' cause and eventually it was agreed. The child would be buried locally.

Yet more people arrived, both Maori and pakeha. The father's family. Two brothers from Australia. Old army mates. They all came because a child had died.

Kenny's mum, Rewa and Ruby were still there, singing and making people laugh even in their grief. Someone knew of a minita and gave him a call. He was from out of town but he came willingly because a child had died.

The last morning and the minita conducted the service. They had to pull the wife and her sister away before they could place the tiny lid on to the tiny coffin and carry her out to the hearse. The road was jammed with cars. There were people everywhere. A father was consoling his daughter who was crying. The old couple from over the road, she who hardly left the house, hanging grimly over a Zimmer frame. The family whose lot it had been to break the bad news. The policeman up at the roundabout directing the traffic. There must have been 100 or more, and they all came because a child had died.

The cortege finally left for the cemetery. The two sisters remained behind to look after things and wait for the minita to come back and bless the house. They heard a noise out the front and went to look.

The dog was standing by the road howling disconsolately. One of the sisters called out but it just kept howling, so she went and took it by the collar to lead it round the back.

It nipped her. Suddenly understanding, the sisters went back inside. The dog remained by the roadside, howling. Desolate in her grief. Her adopted child had died.

The family slept in and didn't stir until nearly 11am the next day, exhausted by grief and all the activity surrounding the death of their little girl. It was while they were eating breakfast one of the children asked: "Where's the dog?" She went to the back door and whistled. When there was no reaction, she went outside to look.

There, under the tree where they would often spread a blanket for the little girl and her canine companion in good weather, it lay stone cold dead.

Mum said it must have died of a broken heart. But shortly afterwards, old Rewa called in and said that they weren't to worry and should be happy, because the dog had decided she wanted to be with the little girl.

This was of great comfort for a family still to come to terms with their loss. But it did leave them with an unanswered question: How had Rewa known the dog had died?

ARMY AND BEYOND

HOW DO YOU WANT YOUR OFFICER BATTERED?

"Okay you guys, sit down, shut your mouths and listen up."

Reluctantly, the platoon slowly quietened and regarded with wary and scornful eyes their new commander standing at attention in front of them in immaculate order even though they were on ops.

They'd heard all about him, of course. He was said to be a lifer, the son of a colonel, a tall, thin streak of a tailor's dummy tipped to go all the way to the top as an officer. He was a stickler for correct dress, bearing and discipline, and apparently he didn't mind tossing the charges around either. Or so the rumour went.

Well they'd soon find out whether that was for sure, because they had him for the next year, the last of their two-year TOD in SE Asia, and the first six of those months would be on active service. And that prospect was certainly something that not one member of the 28-strong platoon, with six months' active service experience under their belts already, looked forward to

"I know you guys think you're good. Well take it from me, from what I've seen and heard so far, you're not, and we might as well get this straight right from the start. I mean to make sure there's a general tightening up of standards around here, beginning right now."

The whole platoon inwardly groaned "oh no". The rumoured bullshit was starting already and they'd only just met the young prick, standing there motionless almost as if he had a raw egg shoved up his arse and was afraid it would break if he moved.

"You've had your orders and should have had your gear packed for Operation Ambush 3 by now, so I want you all lined up back here in 20 minutes ready to move. Before we go I'm going to carry out a full kit inspection".

"Oh god, not a fucking inspection moron." The whole platoon shuddered at this thought.

The officer continued "Now, on the command move double away and make sure you leave your basha area tidy too; I'll be checking on that before we leave. Move!"

To a man not a one of the platoon ran, not even the NCOs. They shuffled away contemptuously and slowly, with a good number shaking their heads sorrowfully. "No! Why us?" was the general consensus.

"Move it you guys! I said double!" barked the lieutenant at the slowly moving backs, but still not a man doubled. The officer's face reddened at the blatant disobedience. "By god," he thought, "I'll have this lot." But he didn't bother yelling again. He certainly had some work to do to get this lot up to scratch.

The platoon sergeant, who'd purposefully ducked attending the parade on the excuse of needing to go to the RAP, had listened surreptitiously from the sidelines and was also thinking along the same path. But about the bloody officer, not the men.

On active service, it was usual for normal military discipline to be relaxed somewhat because they were at times in danger and under considerable stress. They were a pretty well-trained lot and, with few exceptions, good soldiers. Relating to each other on a first-name basis, no matter what rank, created camaraderie and was good for morale, especially in the field.

But this jumped-up little cunt, who in the platoon sergeant's eyes was still shitting yellow, thought he knew better. Well, there was going to be a real problem with morale if the situation wasn't sorted quick smart.

He'd had a quiet word with the lieutenant when he'd first arrived as a replacement for their previous platoon commander, who'd been wounded badly enough to be repatriated. But that had proved a complete waste of time. The officer hadn't appreciated his quiet words of advice and in fact had resented them because he thought he knew it all anyway. He'd been to Duntroon, he'd studied all the training manuals he'd passed all the courses he needed to pass and he certainly didn't need a non-commissioned officer telling him what to do

With that in mind, the sergeant went off to try to find the company sergeant major. Maybe a word from him might help, but he wasn't all that hopeful. He sure wasn't looking forward to the next six months.

The monsoon was late that season and it was blisteringly humid and hot as the platoon bashed their way with great difficulty through the thick secondary jungle.

It had been logged at some stage a few years previously and, of course, that gave all the smaller trees and vines a better chance at the sunlight and they'd all responded remarkably quickly.

The worst part of it was the "wait-a-while", a vine with vicious barbs that seemed to dangle from most of the trees. When it hooked on to your skin, clothes or gear, the only way to get it off without ripping yourself or clothing to shreds was to reverse gingerly, especially if it was in your skin.

Then there were the leeches waving frantically from the leaves or dropping onto the ground once they sensed your presence, desperate to get on to your clothing where they'd crawl till they found a way through your clothes to get at your skin. Sucking on to that, they'd inject an anticoagulant and by the time you found them they'd be that bloated and fat with your blood, they could scarcely move. You couldn't just pull them off otherwise the head would stay in your skin and quickly fester up. You had to get them off by touching them with a lit cigarette or by using salt or insect repellent.

Add to that the ticks, snakes, sweat flies, mosquitos, vicious red ants and myriad other nasty creatures and pitfalls to be found in the vicinity, and you could see that it was not a nice neighbourhood to be in, even with no enemy to worry about.

You couldn't use your machete overly much to aid your movement, either, because the noise which would alert any enemy lurking about and maybe set you up to be ambushed. Generally it was a secateurs-only exercise.

The extremely slow movement pissed the new platoon commander off no end. He wanted to be the first to have his AO cleared or to make contact with the enemy and show the hierarchy just what he was made of.

He'd gone up to the lead section several times already to try and hurry things up. But an angry glare from the lead scout, his clothing sodden and black with sweat, panting with exertion and sporting a couple of angry looking wait-a-while rips on his face, and even the commander had the good sense not to push the envelope.

When travelling through this type of jungle, the person leading had to be changed regularly because heat exhaustion could develop rapidly and often without the victim or his mates even realising. On another occasion when the plonker had gone up front to see what the delay was, the lead scout of the moment hadn't said a word but just pointed to the mass of thick jungle ahead and mutely offered him the secateurs.

The offer was politely declined. Officers didn't bush bash, considering it beneath their dignity. But he was certainly managing to piss the platoon off no end alright. He constantly called O Groups to tell them what they already knew anyway. He made pin-pricking complaints. He checked up on things that were really the responsibilities of corporals or the sergeant, demonstrating his lack of confidence in his men. Morale soon slumped to an even lower level than it was already.

There was even some talk among the platoon hard cases that he might be the first casualty in any contact they had. But hopefully that just more black humour than anything else.

The boys had had their bit of fun with him during his first few nights in the "J" though. Seeing he insisted in sleeping on the ground, they made sure to tell him that some snakes were attracted by human body heat and had been known to curl up next to or even on a sleeping human for their warmth in the past.

Then after stand-down he finally went to bed and was soon unsettled by the B52 bombers, the name given to the huge black flying beetles which flew around at night using their own system of radar to navigate. Unfortunately, they couldn't detect the plastic hutchees the troops used, so every so often there'd be an almighty smash as they cannoned into a one. Very unsettling if you didn't know what the hell it was.

Already amused by the way the beetles were worrying the commander, some of the boys quietly uncoiled some vine near his hutchee site and, after waiting for a while, pulled it noisily through the area. Of course, the platoon was still wide awake and all ears.

He whispered desperately to his sig bashered up next to him: "Hey! Hey! Can you hear that?" But the sig was in on it and pretended he was asleep, although he had great difficulty suppressing his laughter. Next time they did it, his torch had come on, and everyone had sniggered when they heard the sergeant whisper loudly: "Put that fuckin' torch out!"

They'd pulled this gag several times and kept the silly prick awake half the night searching for the elusive snake. He looked pretty washed-out the next morning.

At one of the O Groups, he'd been stupid enough to say he was an officer because he was more intelligent than most and had been born different. He didn't appreciate it when one of the boys asked if that meant he sat down to piss, drawing mocking laughter from the whole platoon. What a dork!

It was late on the afternoon of the second day when the monsoon finally broke, and with a real vengeance. It rained that heavily you could scarcely see, and although it was initially welcomed for its cooling and refreshing effect, it soon added very quickly to their misery, with sticky, glutinous mud becoming another enemy to contend with.

By nightfall, the ground was that soaked and muddy the guys had to use hammocks or make stretchers to sleep on. And the officer was still chaffing at the bit to move faster.

Faster? In that fuckin' jungle and mud? The young fellar might not be an officer's arsehole, but he was surely a good comedian.

By mid-morning the following day, they finally got through the secondary growth but not long after lunch they reached another major obstacle – what was usually a small to medium-sized stream, navigable by canoe and easily waded across in normal times, but now a raging torrent. It wasn't that wide, but the force of the water and the debris coming down would make crossing it a very dangerous, if not foolhardy, exercise.

The sergeant was all for waiting to see if it settled a bit overnight before attempting the move but the platoon commander was in no mood to listen. So they prepared for a rather risky tactical flotation crossing.

The lead section spread out to cover the opposite bank while the second section prepared their gear for flotation and the third section covered the rear. It was all strictly as per the training manual, but much more dangerous than normal because of the state of the stream and the fact that you'd never hear or even see if there was anyone on the opposite bank until someone actually got there to clear it. The platoon would be left very vulnerable to ambush, especially during the initial stages of the manoeuvre.

The sergeant was totally unhappy with the scenario so he went and had a quiet word with the platoon commander and suggested that it would be a lot safer if they put their best swimmer, attached to joined toggle ropes and in clean fatigues, across first. Then he said, the others could use the rope and pull themselves and their bundles across far more quickly and safely.

"Codswallop," said the officer. "I'll show you." Having his gear all ready for flotation, he quickly entered the stream.

"You've still got your boots on, sir!" the sergeant called. But the officer was gone, into the rushing water pushing his bundle ahead of him with rifle tied on top. Of course, he was immediately pulled downstream by the current. About halfway across, when his boots would probably have been filled up with water, he was hit by a madly swirling log, swept away from his bundle, and carried rapidly downstream, fighting to keep his head above water.

He made several abortive attempts to grab overhanging tree branches and even managed to hang on to a slender tree trunk half sunk in the stream for a few seconds, but that soon gave way and he was swept away again, repeatedly being dragged under then bobbing to the surface again

"Dumb young cunt!" yelled the sergeant exasperatedly, but most never heard because of the noise of the river. Meanwhile Fred, the two section commander, and Boy, one of the riflemen, had both already stripped for the crossing and on seeing the drama unfold and clad in only PT shorts and with bare feet, doubled off down the stream bank after their rapidly disappearing commander.

Most of the platoon who saw what happened thought the platoon commander was pretty fucked. The sergeant definitely thought he was about to become fish bait, and a couple of the riflemen, who'd already had a run-in with him and been charged, bloody-mindedly hoped that he would.

There wasn't much the sergeant could do except hope. He cancelled the crossing, got the platoon dressed and assembled again then headed off downstream carrying their absent comrades' gear and thinking they were more than likely looking for a body. He fleetingly considered about radioing base but then thought better of it. The platoon would have to stop moving to put a bigger aerial up and there was nothing base could do immediately anyway.

There was always the possibility that perhaps the idiot might be able to grab a tree or something and hang on, but that was probably a bit of a long shot.

Meanwhile, Fred and Boy were slithering their way as fast as they could along the greasy bank. Being without their gear certainly aided their movement somewhat but they still struggled to make up ground on their leader. Fred had done a good map study prior to going on the op and knew they were somewhere near where the river did a big horseshoe. Suddenly realising this must be the place, he grabbed Boy's arm and pointed into the jungle at a right angle to the raging stream. It realistically was the only chance they had of getting below the boss and perhaps rescue him. The two bare-footed and unarmed soldiers plunged into the lush dark thickness, with wait-a-while vines, snakes, leeches, creepy crawlies, wild animals and even the enemy completely forgotten in the mad dash.

The platoon, meanwhile, moved slowly and tactically down the river keeping an eagle eye out for both friends and enemy. The sergeant was rightly very concerned about his two unarmed men and sincerely hoped old Murphy kept his law in his pocket that day and there was no enemy about.

After a few hundred metres had been covered, the lead scout suddenly stopped and pointed into the river, where the lieutenant's flotation bundle could be seen bobbing furiously in the water, rope snagged over a dangling branch. With the aid of a long stick, it was eventually successfully retrieved, and they were gratified to find the rifle still attached to the end of the rope.

They had his gear and his rifle, but did they still have him?

Some in the platoon claimed not to give a fat rat's arse whether their officer lived or died. But there was always a certain amount of black humour among the ranks at the best of times.

It was a big log that had almost bashed him into unconsciousness which actually gave him a chance. He'd been under and fought his way back to the surface that many times, he had very little energy left. Smashed against rocks, whipped by branches, twisted and turned arse over kite with a bellyful of water and he wasn't too far off chucking it in, when he powered into the big fallen tree lying half in and out of the water.

He was then flung along the side of it and then into a bit of a swirling back-water eddy created by its bulk. Although he was stunned by the impact, his desperate hands somehow found a fork where a branch had been snapped off when the tree fell. With both arms, he grasped and hugged the tree, panting, retching, hanging on for dear life.

Minutes later Boy and Fred burst out of the "J" and stopped. Both were cut and scratched and puffing furiously. They turned and looked upstream, more in hope than expectation. Nothing! Bastard!

Fred, suddenly realised just how vulnerable the two of them were and glanced downstream. He grabbed Boy's arm. About 20 metres away they could see a sodden battered object clinging desperately to a tree trunk.

Boy quickly closed the distance and dived straight in. With three or four quick strokes, he reached the officer turned him and placed his arms around him from the back and began propelling him towards the bank.

Fred, meanwhile, had slid into the water by the base of the trunk and eased his way down to be within helping distance. The semi-conscious officer was in no condition to help but between the two of them, they managed to drag him safely on to the bank where he lay exhaustedly and involuntarily retching, spewing out the water he'd taken in.

He was battered, swollen, cut, bruised and half-drowned, but at least he was alive. They turned him quickly into the recovery position to assist with the exit of the water out of his stomach and lungs. With the tension suddenly eased, the two rescuers burst out in relieved laughter at the sight of the state of each other and then settled down to wait for the rest of the platoon they knew would be following the river down.

They suddenly both felt strangely naked, vulnerable and alone without their gear and weapons, and hoped it wouldn't be too long before the others caught up.

It took nearly two hours before the platoon finally reached the three soldiers, and they were greatly surprised to see their barely recognisable officer alive, though still lying weakly on the ground but a little bit recovered and able to talk by then.

The sergeant quickly deployed the platoon into all-round defence and put sentries out while the platoon medic checked out the three men, first the officer then his rescuers.

One of the officer's fingers was found to be bent at a right angle to the rest of them and at first glance he thought it broken, but then soon realised it was only dislocated. It took three attempts to get it back into place. Platoon medics don't generally graduate on that sort of injury, so there was a lot of pain for the officer plus much humour and suggestions from the onlookers. When the officer was finally able to stand, the sergeant decided to pull back into the jungle about 50 metres and hutchee up for the rest of the day. This would allow the officer time to recover further and they could get in touch with base to report the incident.

Boy, happily clothed and re-armed and having had his cuts and scratches treated, was excused sentry for the rest of that day and was sitting with Fred enjoying a brew when a couple of his fellow soldiers sidled up. "E hoa," one of them said. "What did ya wanna go and save that useless cunt for? Ya shoulda let him feed the fish."

Both Fred and Boy both cracked up at this but through helpless laughter, Boy managed to say: "Well, if he'd a drowned, we da probably a got in the shit for polluting the river." This produced further loud laughter from those who'd overheard the repartee and earned a solid "shut up you guys" from the sergeant.

Later on, reporting to base, they learned that they weren't the only ones inconvenienced that day by a flooded stream, but they were the only ones stupid enough to attempt a crossing. This fact was relayed pointedly to their officer, who had no comment to offer. To give him his due, though, he could have been med-evaced with his injuries, but he stubbornly refused to go.

He was no more than a passenger for the next few days while he recovered from the mostly superficial injuries and, of course, a bit of shock as well. He did notice that the platoon functioned very smoothly under the sergeant, with little talking or O grouping needed. Quite often a nod was all that was required for the men to commence the next routine and the troops somehow all seemed a lot happier and did their work far more willingly than they had under him.

Quite often it does take a visit to the spectre of your own mortality for you to open your eyes to other peoples' views and experience and more especially to those who have probably just saved your life.

The platoon commander may have been a bit arrogant to start with, but he wasn't stupid, and it was really noticeable from then on in he began to listen to the sergeant and corporals. Which of course led to a far happier platoon all round

It was a chastened and a wiser officer who returned to base after the op was over, when the two rescuers were duly officially thanked, and it was mentioned in the report that they had probably saved their officer's life.

He learned a lot from that incident, did the lieutenant, and his man-management skills showed such a distinct improvement from then on he eventually earned the epitaph of "a good cunt", which is probably about the highest praise a soldier can ever offer an officer. Over the ensuing years as he climbed higher in the ranks he never forgot his first ever platoon members and especially the two who'd saved his arse. And he never quite shook off the nick name that the boys had for him after that incident either. He was forever "Fish-Finger Finegan".

ORDERS ARE ORDERS

"The bloody officers and Pioneers have all fucked off home on the piss, so if it's good enough for them, then it's good enough for us. It's no skin off your bloody nose, and anyway we've already collected nearly $400 for the booze. It shouldn't take that long to get across the channel and back again. What's your fucking problem?"

"The problem, Private, is the orders, and because I fucking said so," the Corporal growled, stressing the word 'Private' in an emphatic and determined manner that he hoped left no doubt about who was in command.

The men were all gathered around the Corporal's basha, its covering tarpaulin strung high, doubled up and tied off to mostly stunted island trees. Beneath its shade was a rugged-looking stretcher whose inverted V frame was made of the scrubby timber. The bedroll was spread between two frail-looking saplings that miraculously bore the Corporal's weight. There were also two wonky make-do tables manufactured from interwoven branches and vines, a testament to the spare time weighing heavily on all hands. One table was for cooking, and the other had the radio on it.

The Tilley lamp glowed brightly, throwing huge elongated shadows and casting a green tinge casting through the tightly strung, not quite transparent hutchies. This lent an almost eerie atmosphere to the proceedings.

The Corporal sighed heavily to himself, acknowledging the boredom and discontent in the group of men in front of him because he was bored shitless himself. But he was determined to remain firm in the challenge to his authority.

True, it had all seemed such an excellent idea to start with – conducting assault-craft training for the soldiers who, for one reason or another, had elected not to take their annual leave at the same time as the rest of the company. With an out-of-sight, out-of-mind philosophy being strictly adhered to, they'd been packed off to Pulau Ubin, a small uninhabited island off the coast of Singapore. Here they set up a base camp, with everyone thinking that it would be a relaxing, pleasurable and virtually non-tactical two weeks for everyone. And so it had been. The boat drills usually only took up only four hours in the morning when it was cooler. The rest of the time was generally their own.

The trouble was that apart from swimming, snorkeling, fishing, preparing meals, reading and the inevitable card games, there wasn't a heck of a lot else to do.

After a long and mostly tedious week, the two officers, the two married sergeants and three attached Assault Pioneers-cum-boat operators disappeared rapidly on the Friday night, all heading eagerly back to camp so the married ones could enjoy family life and the rest could sample the delights of Singapore. They'd thoughtfully taken all the outboards with them, immobilizing the two remaining assault craft and "removing any possible temptation", as one of the officers said as he left the Corporal in sole charge of the 18 remaining Privates.

The only other ranker left was the attached medic, Lance Corporal Green who, to put it bluntly, seemed totally out of place among the rough-as-guts grunts. Not only was he slightly effeminate, but he also lacked the confidence to use his rank.

The officers hadn't taken the paddles for the assault craft, believing nobody would be stupid enough to try to paddle across the channel. But they'd completely under-estimated the determination and natural instinct of a bored soldier with time on his hands and a hankering for alcohol.

And to make matters worse, glittering invitingly in plain sight just across the channel, probably not much more than a mile away, were the lights of Pongol Point with its market and myriad stalls, bars and restaurants.

So naturally the soldiers, with inveterate trouble-maker Private

Smart (aka Smart Arse) to the fore, wanted to paddle one of the assault craft across in the dark to buy some beer and then return.

Smart Arse had extra standing among his peers, because he was on his second tour of South-East Asia, had seen active service, and had also worn a Lance Corporal's hook several times before losing it for constant drunkenness, disorderly behaviour, fighting, or a combination of all three. His reputation as a bad egg seemed to have no little attraction for a lot of the younger, more immature soldiers. They hung around him, pathetically eager to be regarded in the same vein.

But paddling over the channel to get some piss was a particularly idiotic and dangerous idea. It was one of the main approaches to Singapore, one of the world's busiest ports. Besides a copious amount of general shipping, there were the huge oil tankers, up to a quarter of a mile long, which made a final approach up this channel before unloading their valuable cargoes. Their crews wouldn't be able to see the low-lying, slow-moving and unwieldy assault craft in the dark. Even if they did, they'd never be able to pull up or veer off in time to avoid a collision.

It was a totally ridiculous and extremely hazardous plan. As far as Corporal Clark was concerned, it was just not on.

"Who the fuck are you to try and stop us anyway?" Smart Arse challenged him. "They didn't say we couldn't go anywhere, did they?"

"Why do you think they took the outboards away, meathead," the Corporal replied resolutely. "They probably didn't think that anyone would be stupid enough to try and paddle across. You're not going and that's that."

Smart Arse turned to his fellow soldiers, wishing that they would be a bit more verbally supportive, and said: "Well, we've decided to go, eh boys, and there's nothing you can do about it." With that, he swivelled suddenly as if to walk down to the beach.

The Corporal immediately gripped him by the shoulder. "You're not going. You're on a charge, Smart. I'm placing you und ... "

Smart spun abruptly about and viciously king-hit the Corporal with a round-house sucker punch no doubt developed during many bar brawls and back-alley fist fights. He used it with great effect on this occasion, dropping the NCO on to the sand.

The momentarily stunned Corporal could do nothing to avoid

two heavy kicks to the head, swiftly administered with army boots. He quickly became unconscious.

The startled medic tried to intervene, but Smart Arse just batted him roughly aside with a backhander. "Get outa my way, ya fuckin' fairy," he snarled as Green fell heavily on to the sand.

Turning to the rest, he said: "Come on boys, let's go. Don't listen to these weak cunts, they don't know fuck-all anyway. If we leave now, we should be back before midnight and on the piss. Who's coming?"

As he strode down to the beach where the two remaining assault craft were dragged well up on to the dry, Smart gave not a thought to what he'd just done or the likely repercussions. It was almost as if there would be no tomorrow when he may have to account for his actions.

About a dozen eager figures followed the trouble-maker and quickly began dragging one of the craft out into the water. Then 10 of them, with eight carrying paddles, leapt aboard and from the almost instant order achieved, it could be gleaned that it all must have been organised previously.

In the sudden rush and kerfuffle, not one of them considered getting a life jacket from where, for security's sake, they'd been piled up in close sight of the hutchies.

"See ya in a couple of hours, you guys," Smart Arse yelled to the ones who hadn't been quick enough to become one of the paddlers, or perhaps, being a trifle concerned about what had just occurred and the repercussions, had hung back.

Once everyone was settled, the rebels began paddling the awkward craft with a will, the non-paddling Smart Arse calling the time. They achieved co-ordination remarkably quickly, because they'd been padding the craft frequently during the drills and on nightly fishing expeditions.

Like Smart Arse, none of the paddlers seemed to take the time to spare a thought about any possible repercussions or the risk involved in what they were about to do. So far as they were all concerned, there was alcohol at the end of the rainbow and that was all that mattered.

The low silhouette soon disappeared into the darkness and out of sight of the seven private soldiers left on the beach, more than one secretly relieved he hadn't been forced to make a decision on whether or not to go. Further back inland, alone, bewildered and out of his depth, the medic tended to the Corporal.

Lance Corporal Green was absolutely terrified. He abhorred violence and nothing in his so-far short army career had even remotely prepared him for anything like this. He also felt rather badly that he had failed in his duty somehow in not being able to assist the Corporal. Of a rather nervous disposition to begin with, he'd always struggled with the physicality of his basic training and had become the butt of many verbal and practical jokes during the intake.

He'd been picked early on not to go the distance but he'd somehow struggled through the basic training and started his medical corps training, where utilising the brain rather than brawn was more the go. So he'd slowly begun to come into his own.

He had easily been the top student on the basic med and advanced courses, and had even been assessed to become an officer. But he decided against that himself, because of his general lack of confidence.

After a short stint in Waiouru, he'd been posted to Burnham. There a shortage of medics – and especially single ones for whom far less organisation and hassle was required for shipping overseas – he'd been offered a plum posting to Singapore with the Battalion.

This carrot was also tendered along with a rather early promotion, and it hadn't taken too much soul-searching before he'd accepted.

He rather enjoyed the work in camp up in Asia, manning the RAP and running the daily medical parades. But he didn't really like it when the Battalion hit the jungle, because then he became one of the company medics, accompanying the Coy HQ wherever it went. This sometimes involved a hell of a lot of jungle bashing with a heavy pack – even more so if there were casualties or illnesses among the platoons, which sometimes patrolled miles away from the HQ. At times, there were no choppers available, and it was always hot, sweaty work linking up with a platoon patient, especially with the extra load he had to carry.

And you were usually totally soaked through with sweat and stinking the whole time you were in 'the J', which he also hated.

Having to carry all his own gear plus the medical equipment he found particularly physically demanding and at times he struggled to look after the patient while on the verge of heat exhaustion himself. But, as his very unsympathetic medical platoon sergeant always quoted when he complained, it was all part and parcel of the deal. You shouldn't have joined if you couldn't take a joke.

Green surveyed his patient and mentally reviewed what he'd done so far: checked the airway and breathing, both okay; turned into recovery position; pulse good and strong. What else?

He got his torch and checked the Corporal's pupils. This was a bit of a worry – they were quite dilated and not reacting to light at all. That prick Smart had given him a fair old bash on the swede. It would be bloody lucky if there were no lasting complications.

He thought about the radio and wondered if he should try and contact base. Trouble was he'd overheard the Corporal saying earlier that comms had generally been pretty intermittent from out here on the ancient 77 sets the infantry were still equipped with. And it was even worse at night, when all they could usually get was generally just a whole bunch of mush.

He'd also forgotten most of his signals training, hardly ever having to use a radio, and he didn't really think any of the remaining soldiers would help him if he did ask. Suddenly deciding he had to try anyway and after one more anxious check of his patient, he went to talk to the remaining soldiers.

"Fuck off, Greenie, why should we help you? Okay, Smart Arse didn't have to boot him in the head like that. But it's done now." The voice came out of the darkness. The medic couldn't quite make out who was speaking.

"The Corporal's still unconscious and he's most certainly got concussion, which can be quite serious you know," he replied. He paused to let that sink in, then added: "Are you going to be responsible if he's more badly injured than I think? He needs to be got to the hospital where he can be properly monitored ASAP."

"Nah, you're just saying that to get us worried." Another voice this time. "He'll be all right. I reckon Smartie didn't boot him that hard."

"Then why is he so deeply unconscious?" Green asked. "You've all done the basic med course. Come and have a look yourself if you don't believe me. You know there's going to be big trouble over this anyway, and especially if he's as bad as I suspect. Smart'll probably find himself getting court-martialled, and very possibly anyone who supported him, as well. "

Green hesitated and waited for his words to sink in, well aware he was now nominally in charge. He desperately wanted to do something positive about the situation, especially with the casualty on his hands. Trying to sound calmer than he really felt, he continued after some 10 seconds or so: "On the other hand, just think about it. Anyone who helps me with the Corporal certainly won't be doing themselves any harm come inquiry time."

Feeling he'd made his point, Green left the beach and headed back to his patient. He could hear low urgent talking and some argument going on as he left. "Good," he thought. "At least that's got them thinking."

He found the patient in the same condition as when he'd left, breathing deeply and slowly but with the pupils still widely dilated and not reacting to light at all. Nor was there any reaction to painful stimulation.

Green fretted. The Corporal really needed to be in the hospital where he could be properly observed. He looked over at the 77 set, wondering about the frequencies and call signs and wishing he'd paid greater attention to his signals training.

Out on the water, the rebels were making good progress and apart from the current constantly trying to drag them sideways, it had been pretty easy going so far. They were nearly a third of the way across and about to enter the far more dangerous mid-channel.

There had been three ships in sight when they'd set off, but they were well gone by now and the channel appeared empty, which augured well for the rest of the trip over anyway.

Some of the guys had got tired paddling from the same position so they'd begun alternating sides. With a couple of spare men sitting in the middle, two paddlers could always be having a break, which was a bit of a bonus as well.

At times, they almost had to stop paddling on one side and correct as the current did its best to sweep them off course, but they were getting used to this manoeuvre now and had it off pat, having carried it out half a dozen times already at least.

Smart Arse was starting to have a few slight doubts about

having bashed the Corporal. He hadn't really meant to. It had sort of happened instinctively when he'd been grabbed and swung around. It was over and done before he'd even thought about it.

"Damn that fucking Clark," he thought. "He knows what I'm like. He should have known better than to grab me like that, especially in front of all the boys. I'd have looked piss weak if I'd just submitted. I could always claim self-defence for the punch, and with witnesses I suppose. But those kicks in the head, they'd be bloody hard to explain away.

"Oh well," he decided with a shrug. "What's done is done. Just have to enjoy tonight and worry about tomorrow, tomorrow."

He called out to encourage the lads. "Should be on the beach within the hour, boys. Grab the beer and head back again. Keep it up."

Maybe he could even talk old Clarkie into having a beer with him when he got back. That idea cheered him as he chanted: "One two three dig, one two three dig, port side lighten up, starboard dig it in."

There was a general groan from the starboard side. "Must be time to change round again," one of them yelled.

"Not yet ya lazy bastards," was the rejoinder from the port side. "You've only been there five bloody minutes."

"Fucking bullshit," moaned the voice from the starboard side. "More like 15 minutes."

What was it that their platoon sergeant had once said? The only thing a soldier was good for was worrying about his guts, what hung from it and moaning about his lot. That was a pretty true statement.

But it was a lot easier to navigate if they stayed paddling in time and kept the way on, so Smart Arse chipped in again: "Okay fellas, keep it up. We'll change round again in five minutes. Not too far to go now." The troops kept at their task with a will, the thought of alcohol the carrot.

The irony of it all was that here he was getting the best out of the troops while doing something they'd been specifically ordered not to and for which they would all probably face disciplinary action.

Back on the island, Greenie wasn't all together surprised when, less than 15 minutes after he had spoken to the men, he was approached by two of the private soldiers, Morris and Albert, who offered to try the radio for him. Morris was actually a platoon sig and Green had seen him doing the odd morning and afternoon sked while they'd been on the island.

"We'll be bloody lucky to raise anyone," Morris said. "We've been having trouble getting comms at the best of times, and there's just too much interference at night. But we'll give it a go anyway. The best time seems to be early in the morning, just after sunrise, and we may well have to wait till then."

"Give it a go," said Green. "If you do get through just say we have a casualty who needs immediate evacuation to hospital, that's the main priority. Don't mention anything else at this stage. We don't want to complicate things over the air. We'll worry about the rest of it all later."

The two privates looked pointedly at each other then set about their work. Within 10 minutes, however, it was evident the weren't going to get through. Even the medic could plainly see it was just a waste of time, so he told them to stop.

He checked his patient yet again. Eyes still widely dilated, non-reactive to light. Still breathing strongly and deeply but not reacting to painful stimuli at all. Green was in a dilemma and didn't know what he should do. He looked at his watch. It was nearly 2200hrs, so it would probably at least another eight hours before they could get comms.

There wasn't really much else he could do real. Paddling the other assault craft across wasn't an option, either. In fact, it would be plain foolhardy. He thanked the two private soldiers and asked them to come back at first light and try again. "I'll remember that at least you two tried to help when the time comes," he said as the two soldiers headed off back to their own hutchies.

Green realised it was going to be a long night. He had a patient to look after, which meant he'd have to stay awake. He was also a touch worried about Smart and the rest when they returned and got a few beers into themselves. Smart was well known in the Battalion as a troublemaker and a bit of an animal when he'd got a few beers on board, so there was no telling what might happen.

Trying to take his mind off his worries, he began recording his observations on the Corporal. Better do everything by the book he thought, just in case. He didn't dare to think much further than that. He was hoping against hope that his patient was going to be all right.

The rebels grounded on the beach at not quite 2300hrs after just over two hours of paddling. They were a couple of hundred metres or so further south of the stores and shops than they had planned, because of the current.

Four of them set off to buy the beer, and Smart Arse suggested the rest drag the craft through the shallows as far north up the beach as they could, to make for easier paddling on the way back.

You couldn't actually see Pulau Ubin in the darkness from where they were, but Smart Arse hoped the guys left back on the island would have the brains to stoke up the fire. They had generally been lighting up at night for brewing up and cooking and smoking their nightly catch of fish. He had a fair idea where the island was, but the fire would give them something definite to aim for.

The soldiers left with the task of dragging the craft up the beach moaned a bit, but most could see the good sense in the suggestion and after the four departed, they set about their allotted task.

Smart Arse and his mates were away much longer than they had expected. The stalls and smaller grocery shops that sold beer at wholesale rates were all shut by that hour so they'd had to go to one of the bars, which of course wanted to charge them full price. It took a fair bit of vigorous bartering before the deal was finally struck, although all four still reckoned they'd been ripped off. But they'd really had no choice. They wanted the beer and the canny bar manager could plainly see that, so drove a hard bargain.

The four mutineers hiked back up the beach to their impatient colleagues and after a few quick words, soon had the beer stowed, the assault craft relaunched and were on their way. In the euphoria and eagerness to get back across to the island and start drinking, no one even thought to have a good look around or check to see if any ships were using the channel. Furthermore, their hike up the beach now meant they were travelling down with and slightly across the current, which made for easier paddling and a faster boat speed. But it also meant any shipping entering the channel was now behind them.

They could see ahead all right but in their haste and because they were making such good speed and wanted to keep doing that, apart from the odd glance aft, no one thought to keep regularly checking carefully behind them. They were mostly concentrating on maintaining the rhythm while paddling and keeping their eyes peeled ahead for the first sight of the island. As far as they were concerned, the sooner they got back, the sooner they could start drinking. And that was all that mattered.

The huge, heavily laden tanker glided almost silently into the channel entrance on its final approach to Singapore before anchoring and having its cargo discharged. They'd been cleared and told that the channel was now empty of major shipping so apart from the possibility of encountering a small local fishing boat, which should know to stay out of the main stream anyway, the crew didn't expect any real trouble.

The radar wasn't registering anything either, so possibly that's why the duty people weren't as alert as they might have been, although the low-slung assault craft would have been extremely difficult to spot, travelling in complete darkness as it was.

Whether it was Smart Arse calling the time or the backchat between port and starboard, the latter skiting because they didn't have to paddle that much due to the action of the current, no one initially noticed the muffled noise of the approaching tanker slowly getting louder.

It was almost surreal when it finally happened. One minute they were paddling happily along, all minds focused on sitting around the fire and drinking beer and no one even considering that they might be in any danger. As the tanker drew closer, the noise became louder and louder until eventually one of the resting paddlers in the centre finally picked up the muffled hum. "Hey! What the hell's that?" he called.

"What's what?" Smart Arse asked.

"Ssh," came the reply. "I can hear something." The soldier turned his head aft and peered into the darkness. There was complete silence for a few seconds as all the paddlers automatically stopped, almost as if they'd been ordered to.

Then, to his utter and complete horror, the soldier's night vision finally registered the huge dark, sinister shadow materialising out of the darkness behind them. "Shit, there's a ship right behind us! Fuck! We're right in the way! It's going to fuckin' hit us." Much panic in his voice.

To his credit, Smart Arse reacted quickly. Quickly glancing back to confirm they were in peril, he yelled: "Okay! Okay! Listen up! Starboard side back paddle! Port side forward! Dig! Dig! Dig! Dig!" The craft began to turn ever so slowly to starboard.

"Right everybody! We've got to get out of the fuckin' way! All together now! Forward! Dig! Dig! Dig!" Smart yelled the commands for all he was worth and everyone bent to it with a will. None of the paddlers had even had time to realise just how close the ship actually was. Both the non-paddlers did, however, and watched dumbstruck as the dark shadow grew ominously larger and larger above them.

"Dig! Dig! Dig! Dig it in!" As the noise of the ship grew louder and louder Smart Arse didn't dare look around either. He knew it was going to be fucking close. He kept yelling at them, knowing that if he didn't keep the paddlers at it, they'd only turn to look at the charging mammoth, and that would be that.

Precious seconds had been lost because they'd stopped, but the assault craft slowly, ever so slowly, picked up speed. The crew dipped their paddles deeply and threw their whole bodies behind each stroke.

Back on the beach, a couple of the soldiers had already grown tired of waiting and drifted back off to their hutchies. The rest eventually lit the fire after finally realising this would give the returning paddlers something to aim for.

Under the Corporal's hutchie, the despondent Green sat next to his patient, checking the vitals every half-hour or so. Condition unchanged. No worse. No better. He still felt somehow responsible for what had happened but didn't know why. He just had this nagging feeling that he was going to end up copping the blame. But what else could he have done? He shifted and wriggled about looking for a comfortable spot, then sighed nervously. It was going to be a long night.

They almost made it. The ship actually missed them by the width of a bow wave. The assault craft skittered crazily down the side of the tanker like a leaf down a gutter during a rainstorm, the backwash off the hull actually helping push it further out of harm's way.

The trouble began because of the two resting paddlers, who'd had nothing to do but watch as the oncoming ship grew larger and larger above them until both were absolutely positive they were going to be crushed beneath its towering hull.

Involuntarily, trying to get as far away from the onrushing danger as they could, they both stood up and moved right to the gunnels on the port side, further unbalancing the already crazily lurching craft. By this time, it had slipped almost a quarter of the way down the length of the tanker and was nearly level with its widest point, but being pushed further away from the hull and into safer waters.

But the combination of the backwash and the movement of the two terrified soldiers was enough to tip over the wobbling craft, and all the occupants disappeared into the briny. The ship continued on its way, the crew happily oblivious to what had just occurred. Even if they had known, they'd never have been able to stop anyway. It took a helluva long time to pull up something as massive as that.

Smart Arse was one of the first to recover his wits. Seconds after regaining the surface and a panicked look-round to see where the tanker was, he yelled: "Over here you guys! Over here!" He realised that if he hadn't been in trouble before, he was a real candidate for the axe now.

"Who's here?" he called. "Is everyone okay?" A quick name check revealed that everyone had made the surface and he heaved a sigh of relief. There was no sign of the assault craft, though. It must have sunk or drifted off very quickly. They had a fair way to go before reaching the island, and the current was already sweeping them along rapidly.

He felt his own boots rapidly filling up with water so gave the order: "Anyone with boots on, take 'em off. And your clothes, too. Looks like we've got a bit of a fucking swim on our hands." He tried to sound light-hearted and confident, as if nearly getting run down by a huge oil tanker and getting pitched into the sea in the middle of a busy channel were an every night occurrence.

After a fair bit of bobbing and splashing around, all boots, pants and tops were off, and Smart Arse gave more orders. "Henderson, you and Froggie are the best swimmers. Hit out for the island. They've got the fire going now, I see. Aim for that and when you get there, tell them what's happened and get them to bring out one of the other boats to pick us up.' The nominated two gave assent and off they went.

"Now, who are the weakest swimmers?" Two voices answered then another piped up: "What about you, Nellie, you fuckin' near drowned on flotation." Despite their predicament, this comment drew several laughs. "That's only 'cos my boots filled up with water," the rather large Nellie protested.

"You should have taken the fuckin' things off then, shouldn't you?" another voice chimed in.

Smart Arse's voice suddenly overrode all the bullshit. "Save your fuckin' energy for the swim," he said, " Let's have two good swimmers with each weak one. If anyone starts getting tired or anything, yell out. We better get going now before the current drags us too far down. Take it easy and don't tire yourself out. Any questions?"

There was none, so off they went all in a group, trying to bridge the gap to safety.

The nine managed to stay close together initially, although every time anyone did look up, the fire on the island never seemed to be that much closer. Smart Arse was encouraging them along for all he was worth. Although resigned to the fact that he was fair in the shit for snotting the Corporal and now for probably losing an assault craft, he remained determined to get them all back safely.

"If you get tired, flip over on to your back and kick. But bloody well keep going, otherwise the current will sweep us further and further down so we'll miss the island all together!" he yelled. Then he became aware that the last group had been slowly slipping further and further behind and were now almost out of sight in the darkness. He breast-stroked back to find Nellie floundering and sinking low in the water, moaning his arse off and claiming he was fucked.

"You're not fucked if you've got energy to whinge, Nellie!" snapped Smart Arse. "Now come on, get over on your back and get on with it, ya useless prick. Smithy, you swim back up to the other group. Harry and I'll stay here and give Nellie a hand." Smith swam off gratefully while the remaining two adapted their stroke and began to haul their big, reluctant comrade rather ungently along.

The moonlight glinted off the water as the soldiers ever so slowly made their way closer to dry land, the only consolation being that because they were in the tropics at least the water was warm.

It was well after 0100 hrs when Green, who had not long nodded off despite his best intentions, was awoken by the damp, nearly naked and bedraggled Henderson and Froggat. "What the hell's going on," he started, but even in the dimming light of the still-hissing Tilley lamp he could see something serious was up, so he shut up and listened.

"Oh shit," he said once he'd heard the bad news. "That's all we need. What'd Smart Arse tell you to do?"

"Come back grab the rest of the boys and take another assault craft out to meet them," answered Henderson. "With us two, there'll be enough to paddle."

"Okay, okay," said Green, thinking quickly and, more surprisingly, all nervousness forgotten. Suddenly remembering his patient, he made a quick visual check that revealed no obvious change in the Corporal's condition. "I can't really leave the Corporal by himself," he said. "Um, Private Froggat what say you stay here and keep an eye on him and I'll go with the boat out, because some of those guys might need medical attention."

Froggat was unwilling. "And what am I supposed to do if something happens?" he asked. "I've only done the basic med course."

"Not much you can do, really" came the reply. "There's been no change in his condition yet. He's still deeply unconscious. You just watch him, keep him in the recovery position just in case he wants to vomit and if he does, make sure his airway remains clear. Hopefully I won't be gone too long."

Recognising the sudden determination in the previously unconfident Lance Corporal, the Private reluctantly agreed. "All right, then," he said, "but don't blame me if anything goes wrong."

"If you do your best, Private, then no one can blame you for anything. Anyway, I don't think there'll much change for a while, by the look of it, at least hopefully not until I get back anyway," Green replied.

Then he turned to Henderson. "Come on then, let's go and wake the others up and get out there." The two disappeared, heading towards the fire, Henderson calling urgently to the others and leaving a rather bemused and bedraggled Private in charge of the casualty.

The two front groups, still quite close together and making reasonable time, were now within a kilometre or so of the island. The weaker swimmers were flagging just a little but were being encouraged along by the others to relax in the warm water and alternately use breaststroke then to flip over on to their backs and kick when they got tired.

They weren't swimming directly against the current, but sort of angling across it, and as it was also having much less of an effect as they got closer to land and out of the centre of the channel, the swimming was becoming that much easier. It looked like they were going to make the island okay.

But the rear group – Smart Arse, Harry and Nellie – were slipping a long way behind the others and getting dragged further and further down the channel all the time. They were in real danger of missing the island. This wasn't such a big deal for the two better swimmers, because there were a few smaller islands further on down and they could both swim and float along with the current till they gained a landfall somewhere. But with Nellie almost panicking, they could see that he wasn't going to stay calm or relaxed long enough to be able to achieve that option.

"Come on, ya useless fat cunt!" screamed Smart Arse. "You're always shooting your mouth off about how good you are! Give us a hand, for fuck's sake. If you help, we'll be able to out of this, but we can't do it if you fight us. Float on your back and kick ya feet. We'll tow ya, all right?" This mouthful of abuse from such an acknowledged expert seemed to quieten and shame the struggling Nellie, for the moment anyway, and the trio resumed their painstaking journey.

The rescue craft was only about 500 or 600 metres out from the island when one of the paddlers reckoned he heard something, so Green had them stop paddling and keep quiet while they all listened. They heard nothing initially, but a yell quickly brought an answer from somewhere much further out in the darkness. They began paddling furiously toward where they thought it had come from, each group sounding off every so often, and eventually they rendezvoused with the lead group of three, soon followed up by a very thankful second group.

The weaker swimmers were heaved on board, sagging damply and gratefully on the bottom of the craft the while the rest hung on to the sides having a well-earned breather. "Where's the others?" Green asked after doing a quick head count. "Smart Arse and Harry stayed back there because Nellie reckoned he couldn't keep going," Smith replied. "He was panicking a bit too, so they might have a bit of trouble there, I reckon."

That wasn't good music to the Lance Corporal's ears and his worries were further exacerbated when no amount of calling brought a reply from the missing group. Green suddenly found himself in the position of having to make a hard decision. There was really no way they could all fit in the assault craft and still continue on with the search. It would make it far too heavy and cumbersome to paddle effectively and then there would be no room for the other three even if they did find them.

Should he carry on looking for the missing three and let the four hanging on to the gunwale make their own way back to the island, taking the risk they were going to make it alright? Or should he escort them back to safety then come out again. He looked at the four soldiers still in the water clinging to the side and asked: "You guys reckon you can make it back okay by yourselves? It's probably only about 500 metres or so to the beach."

The two dubious replies of 'yes' combined with two of 'I dunno' weren't that spontaneous or awe-inspiring and didn't exactly ease the decision he now had to make.

"What the hell do I do now?" he thought. Perhaps joining the army hadn't been such a good idea after all. Then he stood up and screamed: "Smart! Smart!" at the top of his voice. Several times. Several of the paddlers took up the chorus as well, but the calling was in vain. There was no answer. Green slumped dejectedly back down into his seat, decision time had arrived.

"The fuckers could be anywhere by now," came an unwelcome comment from one of the soldiers. "And we're drifting further and further away from the island," came another.

Green agonized for a further few seconds before suddenly making his decision. "Okay," he said. "Let's head back in as quick as we can. We'll get you lot to safety, then come straight back out again." He felt suddenly better for having made his mind up, and there was certainly no argument from any of the others as they eagerly set about the task, most of the swimmers in particular being rather keen to get their feet back on dry land again.

His decision had actually come from the first line of the old adage he was taught as a child by his parents: a bird in the hand is worth two in the bush. Get the ones you've got back to safety, then go back and look for the rest. That seemed like the sensible thing to do. He just hoped it was the right thing.

"Nellie, you cunt!" roared Smart Arse three-quarters of an hour later. "Don't you fuckin' give up on me now, or I'll fuckin' smash your head in when we get back to the beach." Big Nellie was shot, his body sagging lower and lower into the water, barely able to float, his two companions virtually having to pull his whole weight along them and Harry beginning to struggle now himself. "I can't keep going, Smarty," gasped Harry. "I can't keep towing him and swim myself, he's too fuckin' heavy."

Smar Arse, who'd begun to realise that fact from the effort he'd had to put in himself over the last quarter of an hour or so, was in a real quandary. What the fuck were they going to do?

"We've drifted too far down to make it back to the island now anyway, Harry," he said eventually. "Look, there's still some smaller islands further down we can land on. You go ahead by yourself, just keep going across the current, the odds are you'll pick one up sooner or later. I'll follow on as best I can with this big useless lump of ... " He didn't say the word, suddenly remembering whose idea it had been that had put them in their present predicament.

Smart Arse started tugging at the waist of his PT shorts. He sensed Harry wondering what he was doing and said: "I'm going to tie him to me somehow, just in case. Go on, away you go, no fuckin' sense staying here. When you land, yell like fuck. It'll give us something to aim for."

None too sure about the plan but simply too exhausted to argue, Harry slipped away into the darkness, breast-stroking feebly across the current using as little energy as possible because there wasn't that much left in the tank That left Smart Arse alone with his barely floating, totally spent and inert companion.

The assault craft grounded back on the island in the wee small hours, much to Froggy's relief. He hadn't much enjoyed being left virtually on his own, let alone bearing responsibility for an unconscious patient. He had nothing to report, though. The Corporal's condition hadn't changed at all, which was a further worry to a now very stressed Lance Corporal Green.

After a quick check of the patient and delegating responsibility for him to one of the more intelligent Private soldiers who remaining behind, and urging him to start trying the radio at 0400 hrs, he reboarded the craft and they quickly disappeared into the darkness again.

Smart Arse accepted the fact that they in deep trouble. Totally exhausted, he was barely able to keep the almost comatose Nellie's head out of the water. He'd completely given up trying to steer across the current and was just letting it carry the two of them along, with Nellie's body a dead weight and making it harder and harder to keep even his own head out of the water,.

"Hell!" he thought. "Never mind being in trouble with the army, if something doesn't give soon, Nellie might drown. Shit, I might even drown." It was a sobering thought, so he began kicking again but with very little energy as the two were dragged further and further away from any chance of rescue.

On board the rescue craft, they'd clicked on that the current had dragged the still missing soldiers well down the channel, so they begun to paddle furiously that way themselves. They stopped and called out loudly every so often, shining a torch that someone had had the nous to pick up, but there was absolutely no reply. Suddenly there was a general sober realisation that perhaps they had the makings of a real disaster on hand and if so there would be big, big trouble for not a few of them. They all bent to their task with a will, hoping against hope they could locate the three missing soldiers before a tragedy occurred.

But it was too late by now. Far too late for Nellie, who, unconscious and probably already dead, was heavily weighing down Smart Arse and causing the latter to expend all his energy. Smarty could have probably saved himself if he'd cut Nellie loose, but for some inexplicable reason he didn't.

Maybe it was the fact that he was responsible the problem in the first place, or maybe it was just his plain stubbornness and refusal to give in that made him remain tied to his fellow soldier. He stayed with his mate to the end. Whether he even knew Nellie had gone, no one would ever know. But sometime during the next couple of hours, he finally went under for the last time himself. He was an inveterate troublemaker and no hero, but it could be said he did manage something noble in the end.

The lads on the assault craft never did find them, either, and they were still out at dawn paddling their way tiredly and painfully back up the channel to the island after finally realising that the fate of the missing three was now well out of their hands. When they did land back on the island, they found a still unconscious Corporal Clark and the news that the sig had managed to get comms with camp. A helicopter was expected at any time but only really expecting to pick up an unconscious patient.

The sig had only passed on what a now panicking Green had told him to.

Greenie was on the radio trying to explain the situation but still plagued with intermittent comms when the chopper arrived, thankfully with a medical officer on board. While the doctor checked the patient, Green had a quick conflab with the pilots who soon got on the air with their rather more powerful radios.

Realising the urgency of the situation, the doctor quickly decided that his patient was stable enough to delay medevacing while the chopper did a sweep of the area. After a blast of noise and sand, the area turned quiet again, Green and the doctor looking after the patient and discussing the turn of events while the rest of the soldiers sat hopefully, quietly and morosely together on the beach.

They were all extremely worried, especially those who had taken part in the moonlit paddle. No matter what the final outcome, the excrement had certainly hit the cooling device now.

The chopper quickly located Harry on one of the smaller islands further down the channel. He'd crawled thankfully ashore in the early hours, staggered up above the high tide mark and promptly fallen asleep. The mozzies had got at him and his face was swollen badly, but at least he had survived.

After a fruitless further hour searching, the pilots decided to return to the island and airlift the patient to the hospital. In the meantime, a full search and rescue operation had swung into operation on the water.

Later that afternoon, Smart Arse and Nellie were discovered

drifting down the channel, still tied together. That old soldier's enemy, boredom, and a desire for alcohol were the cause of their demise.

Of course, there was a court of inquiry where all sorts of questions were asked, not the least being the propriety of the officers leaving the men with only a full corporal in charge.

That was explained away by saying that it was not an uncommon practice and that Corporal Clark, who had regained consciousness in hospital but was plagued with headaches for months afterwards, had actually been an acting sergeant at the time. Clark couldn't remember a thing about the incident and was shocked when informed that two of the soldiers had drowned

Those who had taken part in the paddle were all eventually charged with disobeying a lawful command, not that serious an offence. But the main culprit was found to be Smart Arse, and since he was dead, he obviously couldn't be punished. So the inquiry didn't really sort that much out at all and was of no consolation to Nellie's family, who still wanted to know why their son had died.

And Green, who was found to have done his best in trying circumstances, still felt that perhaps he could have done more. After his time in Asia was up and having decided that being a soldier just wasn't him, he took his discharge and began studying to become a doctor.

Despite his misgivings, there wasn't really a lot more he could have done that night.

The orders had been disobeyed and as he wasn't up to reinforcing them with violence, what else could he have done? Violence was just not his way.

DON'T SPANK THE MONKEY

Sad to say, but it was generally accepted right throughout the Battalion that the CSM of Delta Company, WO2 David Holt, was a complete and utter first class wanker. A drill pig and cardboard-cutout caricature soldier of Goon-esque proportions, "Dolt" as he had very quickly been nicknamed by the troops of D Company, strutted round the camp as though he had the proverbial egg shoved up his arsehole. But it couldn't have been an ordinary chook's egg, though. Oh no. The way he marched, they all reckoned it must have at least have been the size of an emu's egg, or maybe something even bigger than that.

The creases on his heavily starched greens were so sharp you could probably cut yourself on them. You could become blinded by the sun reflecting off his beautifully spit-polished boots or the dazzle of metal knobs of the drill cane which he kept tucked tightly under his arm, perfectly parallel to the ground, as he marched around camp in exemplary military order at a precise thirty-inch pace, looking for anything that wasn't quite regimentally correct.

There was always plenty to be found. But even if there wasn't, he'd simply make something up. If the rubbish bins weren't in line or didn't look military enough, any soldier unlucky enough to be in the vicinity would immediately be summoned to straighten them up. "Move up the third rubbish bin on the left. That'll do. Stand fast the second rubbish bin. Who told you to move?"

And if he happened to discover a cigarette butt on the ground ... well, what an absolute disaster. Any unfortunate passer-by would immediately be ordered on to butt-picking-up duties. Small wonder that when he was on the prowl, the word filtered round the lines and everybody immediately went to ground.

Dolt had spent most of his career as a recruit and cadet instructor in Waiouru and the general consensus was that he should have fuckin' stayed there. Nothing was ever good enough and even though he was only a Company Sergeant Major, the way he carried on you would have thought he was the bloody Regimental Sergeant Major of the Battalion.

It was patently obvious that this was his ultimate ambition, but the whole Battalion would shudder the day that happened and very probably a myriad discharges or requests for RTNZ would fly in immediately.

He wasn't renowned for a sense of humour, either, as one member of the Company had found out the hard way on the very first day he'd joined them. As soon as he possibly could, he'd marched the whole Company out on to the parade ground for drill "to assess their standard", as he'd said at the time.

He ordered them to line up, with the tallest on the right and shortest on the left, then to number off from the right. One of the Company hard cases, Ted, had been seventh in line and when it came his time to call, he called "bottles", which was a drinking game they often played in the Naafi. Of course, the whole company laughed, which greatly upset the CSM. Ted was charged and he ended up with seven days CB for his trouble. "Bottles."

But you can't keep a good man down. Later that day, when the Sergeant Major had finished briefing them about the high standards he expected them to reach and then maintain, and the fact that they weren't anywhere near them at the moment, he finished off by saying that he understood that there was a thief in the Company.

"In my eyes," he'd warned them, "any soldier who would steal off another is just a scum of the earth, and I will soon scour them out and get rid of them."

After this dire warning, he asked if anyone had anything to say to him. Old Ted, game as ever, immediately stuck his hand up, "Sergeant Major," he said in a mock-aggrieved tone that sounded a lot like the Sergeant Major himself "some scum of the earth has stolen my boots."

Well, the whole Company cracked up at this piss-taking but again Dolt was not so impressed. Being a bit of a religious man, he never swore. but it came bloody close this time. "Fu... come and see me in my office, Private Taylor" he said when he finally managed to wrest control back from the mockingly laughing company.

Ted had another run-in with him shortly afterwards, which ended up with him and two others earning a stretch in the cells. It seemed their paths were fated to cross too often for Dolt's liking.

The Company had been to the range for a qualifying shoot, and on inspection of weapons after cleaning, Dolt reckoned he found two dirty ones. But instead of just ordering the owners back, he ordered the whole section back again at 5pm, when he found another dirty one so ordered them back at 6pm. Again he found a dirty one, so he ordered them back at 7pm. At 7pm he couldn't find too much wrong with a normal inspection, so he opened the butt trap of an SLR – something never done during an ordinary inspection. There, he managed to find what he was looking for – a tiny speck of dirt. So he ordered them all back at 9pm.

It was becoming beyond a joke so Ted, Bill and George didn't bother with the 9pm parade. They went down to the local village and got on the piss instead. They were arrested when they staggered back into camp in the wee small hours, ending up in front of the Company Commander later that day.

The question was duly asked: "Why did you disobey a lawful command from the CSM?" Old Ted, never one to pull his punches, replied: "Sir, we thought the Sergeant Major was being a fuckin' wanker." His two fellow accused nearly fell over laughing, which earned them all another charge on top.

They ended up in front of the Colonel on the more serious AWOL charge and were fined and awarded a week in the slammer. But the whole story soon circulated round the Battalion, causing much laughter at Dolt's expense.

Dolt certainly was a right, royal, regimental dickhead. Old Ted reckoned he probably even rooted his missus in a military fashion. He gave his version of it in the barracks one night, which had them all in hysterics. He put his battle bowler on his head, imitating the head of a penis, and clutching a pair of basketballs at his waistline, imitating a set of balls, away he went.

"Permission to come aboard, ma'am?"

"Permission granted, Sergeant Major."

"Column! column 'shun! Column will advance in full review order with fixed bayonet! By the right, quick march! Stab, one-two-three, in! One-two-three, out! One-two-three, in! One-two-three, out! One-two-three, in!" Ted was bent over, with his buttocks mimicking the action. The boys were cracking up helplessly but he wasn't finished yet.

"Shot over! Shot out! Splash over! Splash out!"

"Permission to withdraw, ma'am?"

"Permission granted."

"Column will retire, about turn! Quick march, left right, left right, left right. Come on! Come on! Don't go soft on me now."

Bloody hilarious, Ted was a natural comedian and mimic and the cause of much hilarity in the Company, but God knows they needed it with that humourless prick for a CSM.

On a whim while out shopping one of the boys, Toby, bought a little spider monkey down at the local market and smuggled it back into camp. Having animals in the barracks was forbidden.

At night, with the hierarchy gone home, they'd both go for a walk round camp hand-in-hand. "There goes Toby and son," everyone would say.

They called the monkey Dirty Harry, after the Clint Eastwood movie, and he used to accompany Toby to the Naafi as well. But unfortunately his liking for beer would eventually bring about an early demise, although not before he'd met the Dolt.

Once a month there'd be a Company Commander's barrack inspection. Accompanied by the CSM, the OC would inspect each barrack room of the soldiers in his Company. Of course, the Platoon Commanders, Sergeants and Corporals would ensure the place was spotless beforehand and generally with the OC in charge and not the CSM (thank goodness) the inspection was a formality and he'd sweep quickly through the barracks, not even bothering to open up lockers or look in drawers. This was much to Dolt's bitter disappointment, of course.

So to hide Harry on inspection day, they'd just put him in Toby's locker where, because it was dark, Harry would think it was night time and he'd sit quiet and not chatter to alert any predator, much as they did in the jungle where they overnighted quietly in the tops of trees.

But for some reason, possibly because he'd become a bit too

domesticated, Harry chatted quietly to himself this time while the OC and CSM were still in the room. The CSM clocked it and immediately asked: "What's that noise?"

"What noise, Sergeant Major?" Toby replied innocently, silently willing Harry to shut up.

The OC carried on, not having heard the noise, and all would have been well had Harry not chattered again just as they were leaving the room. Dolt immediately swooped on the locker, opened it and fuckin' near shit himself when Harry jumped out straight into his arms.

In fright, he flung the monkey on to the bed and then when he'd recovered enough, screamed: "What's that animal doing in my barracks?"

It was a fair cop, I mean Toby couldn't really say "I don't know Sergeant Major" could he? The CSM wanted Toby, the rest of the room and probably Harry too, charged but the OC, who'd had more than a bit of a chuckle at the spectacle, just told the Platoon Commander to make sure they got rid of it.

Imagine the charge for Harry: "Conduct prejudicial to good monkey business." Anyway the boys did a deal with the dhobi wallah who lived in the camp and with the aid of a small monetary incentive; he hid and fed Harry until Dolt stopped making snap anti-monkey patrols.

But poor old Harry, he got to liking his alcohol a bit too much. Because all the boys would buy him a beer when he went to the Naafi with Toby, he'd get rat-arse pissed and then become rather unsanitary when back in the barracks. Because of this, the boys got him a dog collar and chain and used to put him out on the balcony when he had been drinking.

But one night when he was too drunk he slipped over the side. Whether asleep or simply unable to get back up, they never knew, but poor Harry suffered death by hanging. He was buried with full military honours down by the concourse, then the boys adjourned to the Naafi and got wasted in his memory.

Alas poor Harry, I knew him well. He had a good job, though, and he was well thought of in the monkey business.

Dolt had a real Achilles heel and it didn't take long for the Company to discover it:

He was not a bush soldier's arsehole. He hated going into the jungle and staying in the same clothes for weeks on end, sodden with sweat and remaining dirty and smelly with no opportunity for a wash, and being bitten by all sorts creeping, crawling and flying insects.

After a week or so in "the J", everybody stunk. But after a while you couldn't really smell yourself or the others, probably because you were all the bloody same. There was also some sort of theory that the sweat mixed with dirt formed a film over your skin that protecting you from some of the blood-sucking predators. It was an unproven theory to say the least.

You didn't use soap or clean your teeth with toothpaste, because the enemy might smell them. You could clean your teeth with salt if you wanted, but most of the guys didn't bother, preferring to keep their salt to replace what they were losing all the time. If you're dirty, you're dirty. So enjoy it.

Dolt definitely did not like being in an unclean state and would do everything in his power to try and avoid it. But sometimes he simply had no choice and had to jungle-bash along with the rest of them.

On one occasion, the Company was going to take over a prominent hill in the middle of their AO and dig into stage two, which was a fighting pit for two men, about chest deep. Once the Company position had been completed and fully fortified, they'd send out recce patrols to search for any sign of the enemy.

A Company move is always a cumbersome affair and, after being dropped off early in the morning, it was getting along to about 3pm when they reached their final goal. Digging in had to be completed as soon as possible, and they were going to have to work throughout the night if necessary. When the position had been finally sited to the OC's satisfaction and sentries mounted, digging commenced in the rapidly darkening gloom.

Alongside his natural mimicry and comical talents, Ted was probably the best lead scout in the Battalion. Having been brought up in the backblocks, he had done a lot of hunting and farm work from a young age. So he was no stranger to the art of digging. Neither was his cover scout, George, who was one of the best shots in the Battalion and a first selection for any shooting competition. They made a good pair, those two, with Ted leading the way and George, who could reputedly shoot either eye out of a mosquito from 50 paces, covering his arse.

The pair set to work with a will and despite having to pull sentry duty for an hour each as well, had their pit dug and as well cammed up as they could in the dark just before midnight. The final finishing touches would be added after stand-down the following morning. They had just spread their bedding out and had lit hexamine in the bottom of the pit for a brew when up rumbled the Dolt, with a bloody torch on of course.

"What are you two up to?" he demanded.

"We've finished our pit, we're having a brew and then we're going to have a gonk," Ted replied.

"You can't do that while the others are still working," said the CSM. "Get yourselves over to Company HQ and help with their pits."

Though knowing it would do no good, Ted remonstrated with the CSM. "Sergeant Major, we've finished our pit because we worked hard, and we've also had our turn on sentry. I think we've earned a break."

"I don't care what you think, Private! You're not sleeping while others are still working! Get over to HQ now!" With that, Dolt carried on round the perimeter.

"You can't argue with a brick," said George when he'd gone.

"Prick, not brick," replied Ted, and the two sloped off unwillingly toward HQ.

"Dolt hasn't even started his fuckin' pit yet," said the sig, shining his torch on its outline.

"Typical, the lazy prick," replied Ted. "Come on, George." He grabbed a shovel and started in on it. Ted got stuck in for about 10 minutes before George took over. While he was working, he heard Ted fossicking around in the dark with something. But he didn't pay too much attention.

When they changed over again, he was surprised when Ted handed him a half tin of fruit salad. "Gee, thanks bro," he said and ate while he rested. Soon it was his turn in the hole again and when they changed over, Ted offered him another half tin of fruit. "Cheers bro. You bring plenty, or what?" he asked.

"Yeah, no sweat," replied Ted, and the two kept alternating. When Dolt did finally came back, his pit was nearing completion. "All right you two, you can return to your own position now," he said without even a word of thanks.

The two sloped off shaking their heads. They'd be lucky if they got two hours sleep before morning stand-to.

It wasn't until after stand-down the next morning that George found out about the truth about fruit. They both overheard Dolt coming round the perimeter asking: "Where's Taylor and Higgs?"

"Quick," said Ted, signalling George into some dead ground just outside the perimeter.

"What's wrong?" asked a perplexed George.

"That fruit," said Ted with a laugh. "It was out of Dolt's pack and I filled the tins up with dirt and put 'em back in there."

"Ya fuckin' wanker," laughed George. "He's gonna get us now."

Get them he did. Automatic volunteers for any extra duties, they dug the Company shithouses, they did clearing patrols, they went out on water parties - you name it, they got it. Dolt's revenge kept them very busy for the next week or so.

Actually the whole Company was kept very busy during this period, with reccies then aggressive fighting patrols being sent out in all directions and sometimes staying out for two or three nights lying in ambushes.

While Dolt made sure George and Ted got more than their fair share, it was while out on one of the clearing patrols with Dolt in command that Ted managed to get a bit of their own back.

He'd spotted a hornets' nest on a slender tree on a ridgeline on a previous patrol and having Dolt with them on this one gave him the chance. Hornets were real bastards if you upset them they'd chase and sting the heck out of you. Not just one of them, though. They seemed to attack in formation and they hit you hard. It wasn't unusual to be stung by five or six of them at once. and it was much worse than a bee sting. In fact, it had been known for people to die from an allergic reaction to them.

When the clearing patrol led by Ted moved up the ridgeline and became level with the hornets' nest, he stopped and signalled George with a closed fist on top of his head. Thinking Ted may have spotted something, George closed quietly and alertly. When Ted pointed to the hornets' nest, George nodded but then couldn't believe it when Ted suddenly kicked the tree and dived straight off the ridgeline into the darkness of the jungle below. There was nothing he could do but follow.

It was three quarters of an hour before five of the six-man patrol finally managed to get back together again, with Dolt still missing. The other three had each been stung a number of times, and the Corporal said: "Higgs, Taylor, I'm sure you're responsible for this. Go and see if you can find Dolt."

The two filtered quietly and slowly through the jungle, not wanting to attract the enraged hornets' attention, and finally found their CSM sitting on the track. He'd been hit five or six times in the side of the head, which was now badly swollen, and he was already a bit delirious. He was obviously in no condition to travel, so they had to call in a chopper to get him winched out.

While they were all happy to see him go, they almost felt sorry for the poor bastard. Almost.

George kept Ted's secret about what had actually happened but his silence earned him more than a few beers when they got back to camp. The rest of the OP was a breeze, with no Dolt to worry about.

Dolt ended up in hospital on a drip for a few days before doing back to work on light duties. He was soon on full duty, though, and making a nuisance of himself around camp, bugging the LOBs.

About a week after the hornet incident, Syd from 14 Platoon developed toothache. You know what it's like when you get a toothache: You can't eat, you can't concentrate, you can't sleep. That could be very dangerous scenario not only for the victim but also for the rest of the Platoon when you're supposed to be on the alert looking for enemy. Anyway, a chopper was coming in to bring rations and ammo, so his Platoon commander lined him up to go back and get his tooth fixed.

"You get back to camp, have a shower, clean your teeth, change your clothes then get straight up to see the dentist, and I want you back out here on the first available chopper tomorrow, you understand? No going on the booze and causing trouble!"

"Yes, sir," said Syd.

When you've been living in the J on hard tack for a few weeks, then go back and have fresh food and alcohol, your system has low tolerance – especially for the booze. More than one soldier had completely lost the plot in that situation.

When Syd got off the chopper back in camp, who should be waiting there but Dolt.

He found out what was going on and immediately countermanded the Platoon commander's orders. "This chopper is going back out again in about two hours," he said. "Never mind about a wash and cleaning up! You go to the dentist now, and then you can go straight back out again. I don't want you staying in camp and causing trouble."

"Sarnt Major, I stink and haven't cleaned my teeth for weeks!" protested Syd, whose teeth were actually green. He could see the possibility of much-anticipated fresh food rapidly disappearing.

"Never mind that," replied Dolt. "Just tell the dentist that I sent you, and when you're done come back down here immediately."

So old Syd, stinking like hell and with green teeth, finds himself in the dentist's chair as is. The dentist wasn't really a military man, but a professional given an officer's rank for the duration of the tour. He was well known for his love of rugby, having a beer with the boys afterwards and a rather outlandish sense of humour. Doc, as he was known through the Battalion, bustled into the surgery and saw stinky old Syd sitting in the chair. "Doc," said Syd. "Look, I'm sorry. I've been in the jungle for a few weeks but the CSM wouldn't let me get cleaned up or clean my teeth."

Seemingly not at all perturbed, the dentist replied: "That's all right. I just had a shit and didn't wash my hands."

"Yuck"

The boys cracked up when Syd got back and told them. He was a fuckin' hard case that dentist.

Eventually the OP ended, and they headed back to camp, where Dolt was eagerly awaiting them of course. When the rifles and all the gear were finally cleaned to his standards and correctly stowed, away it was off to the lines and a very welcome shower. That was when you found out how stink you really were.

After the shower, everyone would parade by their bed in PT shorts and jandals. The Company medic and Platoon commander would come around and check that nobody had any sores or pesky varmints infesting their private and hard-to-see bodily parts. It was called an FFI, for free from infection. Ticks and leeches especially had a habit of getting into hard-to-access crevices and even if you did scratch them off the heads would remain under the skin causing a nasty infection.

The inspection involved dropping your dacks in front of the medic and letting him examine your harder to access parts. Of course, he wore gloves and used a wooden spachelor to move certain objects around.

Being the bloody nuisance he was, Dolt somehow always managed to involve himself on this inspection as well, and it went reasonably well and quickly till they got to Hainsy, who refused to drop his dacks.

"Look sir," he said to the Platoon commander. "I'm all right. There's nothing wrong with me. I've checked."

"Come on Hainsy, the medic's got the whole company to do. Why should you be any different? Drop your dacks now!"

"Sir, I promise you, I'm good. There's nothing wrong with me."

Of course, old Dolt just had to become involved. "Take those shorts off, Private Hains, or I'll charge you."

Old Hainsy was a bit of an odd carrot, a real loner, and he seemed to spend a lot of time in Bugis Street where for a monetary consideration the beautiful women would conduct certain ministrations upon your body. Hainsy was a good soldier, though. He had balls, figuratively and literally. But so did all those beautiful women down Bugis Street.

They gave good blow jobs, though. Apparently.

Anyway, eventually and reluctantly, Hainsy did drop his dacks. Two things were patently obvious: He was quite well hung and he had probably three-quarters of a silly on.

Dolt was absolutely disgusted. "You filthy animal, Hains!" he screamed. "You're on charge!" But the medic and the platoon commander were chuckling, as were Hainsy's room-mates, and the threat came to nothing. What would he have been charged with anyway? Flying the flag at half-mast? Failure to maintain rigid military discipline?

I don't think having a silly on is a chargeable offence is it? Maybe in a church, convent or seminary, perhaps. But poor old Hainsy, he never lived that down because he was nicknamed Hard-on from then on.

Then they came to Jack Key, whose nickname was Donk. He wasn't called that because of his surname, although it helped. In fact, it may have also helped if he had had four legs instead of two to carry around what he was burdened with. Put it this way, in the communal showers in the WWII-era barracks back in Burnham, no one liked showering next to him. It was sort of like a grass snake alongside an anaconda. Some blokes get all the luck. Dolt generally always took off before they went into Donk's room and the boys reckoned because it probably reminded him how small his one was.

Dolt was a fuckin' idiot, all right. Several senior people had tried to talk to him about his attitude towards the troops but he just couldn't see it. Instead he was in charge and it was all about them bending to his will.

But it all blew up on him one Saturday morning when the other Companies were stood down for the weekend. Dolt had decided his Company's drill was not up to scratch and ordered a parade for nine o'clock on Saturday morning followed by two hours of drill.

A lot of the boys had been on the booze the night before and weren't feeling that clever and Rob was still bloody pissed. Later on he would say that he couldn't even remember getting home, let alone going out onto the parade ground.

After about half an hour of unsatisfactory drill, Dolt had them halted at attention while he berated them for their sloppy performance thus far. Right in the middle of this, Rob must have finally had enough and he sat down in the middle of the formation. As Dolt began to rave at him, a spontaneous reaction took place. Ted, standing immediately behind Rob, suddenly sat down, closely followed by George. Then slowly, one by one, the others followed suit until the whole Platoon was sitting.

Soldiers in the other two Platoons saw what was happening and followed along. A reluctant few needed to be urged by their mates but eventually everyone was sitting down, leaving only the Corporals and Sergeants still standing. But tellingly, none of these actually turned to tell their Platoon to stand.

Dolt abused them for a full five minutes. He bullied, he screamed and he threatened. Eventually he even cajoled, but it simply had no effect. They'd finally had enough of him and gone on strike.

Realising he was having no effect at all and that they weren't going to listen, and after muttering something about a mutiny, he walked off the parade ground a broken man. The whole Company cheered and clapped riotously.

After a few minutes, one of the Sergeants addressed the sitting men: "All right, you've had your victory for now. But you'll probably hear a lot more about this. Now let's show them we're not a complete rabble and march back to the Company lines and fall out."

With that the striking soldiers slowly got back to their feet and were marched back to Company HQ. After been cautioned about leaving camp, they were fallen out.

Rumours flew around the place that weekend about charges and courts martial, and even the whole Company being placed under arrest. Nothing ever eventuated. There wasn't enough room in the cells for them all anyway.

Several high-powered conferences took place behind closed doors the following week, after which Dolt found he was posted sideways as housing NCO. Delta Company then found themselves with a new CSM with a far different attitude than the last one and the morale improved remarkably quickly. His first words were: "I don't give a fat rat's arse what's happened in the past. Let's work together and show people just how good we really are." And it happened.

Nothing much was ever said about what occurred on the parade ground that day and it certainly didn't happen again. I think the words "mutual" and "respect" were missing somewhere in the mix for a while.

On RTNZ, Dolt got out and became a minister of religion, which was probably a good place for him. He'd have to be a hellfire and brimstone preacher though wouldn't he? Imagine him in heaven parading the angels. "One feather out of place and you're down the stairs to Old Nick." Or perhaps singing: "Marching in the slaves, marching in the slaves, we shall come rejoicing marching in the slaves."

But I mean everybody's got to be good at something, don't they? It's just that sometimes some of us spend our whole lives trying to find out what it is. I know I have.

But what if you were good at nothing or a good for nothing your whole life? What would your epitaph be? "He never did anything useful in his life but he made a fuckin' good corpse?" I know I've worked with people like that. They spend their whole working life practicing to be a corpse. I've even worked with an Australian who, when I berated him for reading a book while we were busy, replied: "Why should I work? I'm Australian!"

SHIT A BRICK

Twelve Platoon moved silently and efficiently into all-round defence, went to ground and stood to. This involved being totally motionless and quiet for 10 minutes or so, observing your arc and listening carefully to see if you were being followed, or see or hear if anyone else was in the general vicinity. It had been quite a hike to get into their AO because they had been dropped off four days' walk away in an attempt not to give their presence in the neighbourhood any early publicity.

Luckily there were plenty of small streams running throughout the area, because they were rationed for 10 days which meant carrying a lot of freeze dries, or "lurps". While these had the advantage of being light, they had the double disadvantages of requiring a lot of water and not having a hell of a lot of goodness in them. Some of the guys reckoned you could starve to death if you were surviving on them. Although they weren't quite that bad, after a few days of jungle bashing, sweating your arse off and subsisting mainly on lurps, you certainly were considerably down on energy. Adding to the misery, you quite often broke out in boils, which could be a very painful experience depending on what bodily part was affected. Another disadvantage of the lurps was they could tie you up badly, leaving you unable take a crap for a week or more, and then when you did it was as hard as fuckin' bricks and the cause of a real muck lather in the effort to snap one off. It did cause a bit of mirth amongst the boys at times, watching one of their mates balancing delicately over a hole in the ground struggling to snap one off but often only being able to manage an extremely loud and somewhat odoriferous fart. But then, when you are under serious pressure, anything even slightly comical can seem that much funnier, can't it?

Reports had come in to HQ about guerrillas using a rough track through the jungle at night and going into the scattered villages to harass the locals, demand food and, on occasion, abuse the women. This latter fact was probably why the normally tight-lipped inhabitants made a complaint in the first place. Not only would curing the problem be doing something positive for the locals, a sort of hearts and minds thing, but also it was also a chance to get rid of a few unwelcome and somewhat parasitic immigrants into the neighbourhood

Twelve platoon's task was to find a likely spot along the track, set up an ambush and then wait hopefully for someone to walk into it. Because there was a strict curfew after dark for the locals, theoretically any encounter would be only with the enemy. The platoon stood down after the clearing patrol had quietly circled and cleared the area directly in front of the platoon's triangular shaped perimeter, and each of the section commanders had placed a sentry out directly in front of their own gunner's position. Then a patrol, comprising the platoon commander, his sig, one of the section commanders and his 2IC plus their lead scout and machine-gun team armed with an M60 and an SLR, moved forward to reconnoitre the track the enemy were supposedly using, reckoned to be only be about 100 metres or so forward. The rest of the platoon sat quietly observing their arcs, grateful for the respite after four days of solid walking.

The patrol soon cut the track and while the machine gun team and the section 2IC covered an end each, the officer and the section commander planned the ambush, deciding where they'd place the gun and the claymores for best effect, and where the cut-off groups would be positioned. This task was soon completed, again very quietly and efficiently, and while the officer and his sig moved back to the platoon harbour, the gun team and 2IC kept watching the track. Using secateurs, the section commander and his scout began clearing a path from the ambush site, so moving back and forward would create minimal noise.

When all was ready, the officer called an O Group and gave the orders to his sergeant and the section commanders, who then in turn passed them on, with stealth and quietness the keynote. As it was now getting on to late afternoon, the two sections who would man the ambush on the first night had a quick meal before moving forward to the site. Then with a quick burst of hectic activity, the claymores and trip flares were set up and camouflaged, the two two-man cut-off groups were positioned and the section gun located to give the best possible coverage of the killing ground. Once all was completed, the 2IC of 1 Section and his gun group, who had been covering either end of the track then withdrew back to the platoon.

The ambush was set. The flares were on a tripwire so anyone walking down the track would set them off, but the claymores were command detonated. The claymore clackers, the switches that would send an electrical impulse down the wire to the detonators, were sited at the machine gun where the section commander and his four men would take turns manning them during two-hourly stints on the gun overnight.

The section 2IC and his offsider in the first cut-off position were both armed with a 7.62mm SLR, favoured over the 5.56mm M16 for its knock-down power, and the two soldiers in each of the other two cut-off points, only 20 metres or so either side of the kill group, were similarly armed. These men would have to do two hours on and two hours off overnight, but it would be hard to relax enough to get any sleep being that close to the track. If anyone was spotted or heard by any of the cut-off groups a tug on joined toggle ropes would alert the people in the kill group. If nothing happened overnight, then 3 Section would take over after first light the next day, and then 1 Section the following night, and so on, depending on how long it went on for. Eventually everyone would get their fair share of the day-and-night routine.

It could become very boring just sitting or lying on the ground right next to each other, so just by reaching out a hand you could alert your mate with minimal movement or noise. No bedding and no mozzie net – you'd be dive bombed by the little fuckers all night. Various other nasties were about as well, including snakes and wild animals in all likelihood. Having to keep quiet and motionless for hours on end and not even being able to smoke was even worse, so everyone hoped whatever was to happen would go down bloody quickly.

Meanwhile, the rest of the platoon carried on with the normal routine: sentries out, including one to cover the vacant sentry spot left by the absent 2 Section. However, all had to remain ready to move immediately the ambush was sprung to do a sweep through the area and maybe follow up any enemy who'd managed to avoid being killed during the initial firefight and escaped.

The first night passed peacefully enough with no enemy activity, so after stand-down and a hasty breakfast, 3 Section replaced 2 Section for the day-time stint removing the trip flares immediately after taking over the ambush. They would not be needed during the day, and could possibly be seen by an alert enemy. They would be replaced again just before last light when 1 Section took over the ambush for the night. Two section then returned back to the platoon area for a brew, a scanty feed and, with a bit of luck, a catch-up on sleep as well, but still remaining ready to move in an instant. Although the enemy weren't expected to pass through during the day, you never really knew and had to be ready for anything and everything.

That day passed quietly by and just before dark, 1 Section took over the ambush for the second night. Again it was a fruitless vigil and the sections changed again for the day shift, quickly and with little fuss. It was all becoming second nature by now but also very boring.

Luckily there was a small, clear, fast-running stream nearby, so water wasn't a problem. But food was a problem – or rather, the lack of it. When you've got time on your hands and nothing much to do, the mind does tend to turn to food, which there wasn't a lot of. What there was, was pretty fuckin' tasteless. Some of the guys tried spicing up the lurps by adding curry, chilli, Worcester sauce or even onion, but it still tasted like shit, and not moving wasn't helping promote healthy bowel action either. In fact quite a few of the guys had already become constipated and no matter how hard they tried, they were only able to emit loud foul-smelling effusions, much to mirth of those who were unfortunate enough to be within hearing and smelling distance. Still, laughter did help keep the morale up.

The third night passed with no action and the changeover was made again just after first light. The platoon had been out six days now and had seen nothing. A few souls were even beginning to switch off a little, which could be dangerous and something to be avoided at all costs. The day passed and for the fourth night, 2 Section manned the ambush again, but this time with the sergeant in command. He'd grown bored staying in the platoon harbour and decided to give the section commander a break for the night and took his place.

Things proceeded normally until about 0143hrs when one of the men in the kill group, who'd actually somehow managed to get off to sleep, let off a horrendous great fart, loud enough to be heard by both the cut-off groups. Of course, it had to be old Blaster, named and famed for his ability to fart virtually on command and loudly at the best of times, let alone when tied up on lurps. Back in NZ, he'd actually been the subject of an official complaint by one of the WRACs to the orderly officer. "That man," she'd said, "that man just sits there and farts while we're eating, and says nothing."

Apart from the sergeant, everyone else could barely contain their laughter and each could feel his nearest neighbour shaking helplessly in the dark. The sergeant whispered "shut up you guys" loudly several times, and shook Blaster awake. He couldn't understand what the hell was going on or why everyone was quivering with barely suppressed mirth.

Things had then settled down for a further 15 minutes or so when one of the cut-off group guys suddenly let one rip, closely echoed by a really loud answer from Blaster, on purpose this time. Now they were all rocking with laughter again and the sergeant's loud whispered "shut up you guys" several times was totally ignored as several others joined in to a chorus of a mad few minutes of loud farting and barely suppressed laughter. You could say it was a release of pressure in more than one way and it took a quite a long while for the helpless shaking to cease and the sergeant to regain some sort of control.

The rest of that night passed uneventfully and first thing in the morning the platoon received word to withdraw from the ambush and head back to where they could be picked up by choppers and returned to base.

As usual on arrival at base and after the clearing of weapons, it was a hot fresh feed with heaps of bread, butter, sauce, plus a can of beer or coke per man. Then it was the cleaning of the gear, more especially the weapons, every soldier's lifeline. After this was complete it was straight into the shower and you generally only realised just how stink you'd been when you were showered and back in clean clothes then had to put the dirty ones into the dhobi. They absolutely reeked. Then it was into the debrief, which lasted nearly two hours, and finally they were free to have a few beers before tea and maybe a few more after.

Reveille was not welcomed at all the next morning, with more than a few nursing hangovers plus some with the shits, the beer and the change over from lurps to comparatively rich fresh food the prime cause. At about 1100hrs the platoon commander was called to a briefing on their next task, so the sergeant took it upon himself to have his own debrief about the ambush, or rather the noise that had been made in it on the last night.

"Listen up you guys," he said to the platoon dressed in PT shorts and singlets and sprawled out in various postures on the ground. "That was bloody bullshit the other night. I mean, I know the lurps tie you up but you can't be doing that sort of shit in an ambush. You could compromise the whole operation."

"That's the thing, Sarge," Ben called out. "If we could have a shit, then we wouldn't be doing that shit would we?"

The crack bought general laughter from the platoon, and then Blaster added: "Sarge, if you have to fart, you have to fart. It's a natural thing, isn't it?"

More laughter and the sergeant replied: "Nothing natural about you, Blaster. You're a sick man. You need to go and see the gunners to get your arse reamed out. And I reckon you should pay the dhobi wallah danger money for washing your cruds."

The platoon all cracked up at this little pearl of wit and when he finally got control back, the sergeant continued.

"Look, if any enemy had been coming along the track, they'd probably have smelled or heard us from at least 100 metres away. If you find you really do have to fart when we're in a position like that, then at least do it tactically."

This comment brought even more laughter and Ben, thinking it was a joke, called out: "How the hell do you fart tactically, Sarge?"

But no. "You stand up and bend over like this," the sergeant demonstrated. "Spread your cheeks to open up your anus as wide as you can and then the gas should come out a lot more quietly."

His face grimaced as he put in a big effort to try and produce enough wind to demonstrate his theory. But he had forgotten one small thing. They were no longer on lurps and had had three fresh feeds plus alcohol to boot. Quite enough to loosen up even the most recalcitrant bowel. Suddenly, following an almighty explosion that sounded something like a loud ripping noise, the sergeant shit himself. The loose watery stools with the odd lump visible poured from the inside of his PT shorts like a lahar down a mountainside. He turned and began to walk stiff-legged away toward the latrines, legs spread wide apart as if trying to limit the downward flow.

The whole platoon sprawled helplessly on the ground pissing themselves with laughter.

The platoon commander turned up half an hour or so later eager to give a warning order for their next task. He couldn't find the sergeant who was probably still in the latrine rinsing his cruds out and he could get absolutely no sense out of the rest of the platoon. They were all still laughing and jabbering like a troop of monkeys high in the trees after having successfully avoided predators overnight and now first thing in the morning excitedly letting the world know that they were still alive.

In total bemusement at the unbridled hilarity, he decided to postpone the briefing session till the following day.

INSTINCTIVE TARGET

For Dick, a fellow ex-soldier, friend to Poi and me, plus adviser, kaumatua and all-round thorough gentleman. Aye, Tikirau.

Ray Weston squarely faced one fact: Lethargy, boredom and lack of interest almost inevitably took root on any employment he had ever attempted since getting out of the army. Being back in Civvy Street had never really suited him, he reflected. Being brutally honest with himself, he thought he was probably just a misfit, somehow never quite adjusting to the humdrum existence of being a plain, ordinary mister, even though he'd been discharged from the army going on for four years now.

He was 58, although he looked a fair bit younger even if his face was slightly battle-scarred, courtesy of rugby, a bit of boxing and the odd bar brawl up in Asia. He was just above average height but with a solid, stocky build that made him look rather shorter than he actually was.

He'd made a point of keeping himself as fit as a buck rat since he got out, however, because he always reckoned he got fat just looking at food and had also observed too many of his fellow soldiers running into medical problems after taking their discharge from the army. The trouble was, they would continue to eat, drink and live their lives as hard as if they were still in the military, but neglected to do any of the hard physical work or exercise that they would have done had they still been there.

Reports of old comrades dying of heart attacks or developing some sort of disease or other were reaching his ears all too often these days, especially among the Vietnam vets. For his own part, he badly missed the vicarious thrill of doing something dangerous enough to cause the scalp to crawl, raise goose-bumps all over the body or make the sphincter muscle tighten entirely involuntarily. He had to face the fact that he had loved the life, the living hard, the constant risk-taking and nerve-testing, and life without it was basically as boring as shit.

So it was understandable that he had found it extremely hard to find work that even remotely interested him once he'd quit the army, as evidenced by the numerous jobs he had had since taking his discharge. He'd soon found that most of the bosses or supervisors had absolutely no people management skills. And a goodly percentage of his fellow workers couldn't work in an iron lung. That old army joke – "Take your boots off." "Why?" "So you're easier to carry." - applied just as much in Civvy Street as it had been in the army, probably even more so. At least the army had weeded out most of the bludgers, eventually

Considering that he had clocked up some 30 years of service in the army, beginning as a teenager and seeing action in two Asian wars, it was probably no wonder he'd had some trouble in adjusting to a more sedentary lifestyle. Ray's service had also cost him two marriages along the way, the first because his wife of 11 years and mother of his three kids had finally grown sick of him being away for up to six-to-nine months of the year and had eventually issued an ultimatum: Her or the army.

He'd tried hard to reason with her, saying that he had already been in the army when she'd met and married him and had been well aware that he'd be away often. He also pointed out that the army had always sent people around to see if the family needed anything when the husband was away for long periods. But she'd just spit straight back: "Yeah, and half the guys they sent around to mow the bloody lawns wanted to mow my loins instead. I'm sick of living like a bloody widow all the time. It's me or the army, your choice."

He couldn't argue too much. It was basically true – he was away a lot. But he hadn't been too far off a pension for 20 years' service and it didn't seem to make sense to get out early and lose all the accumulated benefits. He'd tried his level best to win her over. Even the battalion commandant, who didn't want to lose a good and experienced senior NCO, tried to help by offering a two-year posting to the garrison battalion in Singapore for the whole family. This was an eagerly sought after perk, the overseas allowances making for an excellent standard of living in Asia and bringing into reach luxuries that were generally unobtainable in New Zealand. But it was all to no avail. Her mind was made up. After much troubled and deep soul-searching, he decided he was really unwilling to give up his army career. It was the only life he knew.

So the marriage had ended on a somewhat bitter note, costing him a house and a fortune in child maintenance for the three kids over the next few years. Thankfully they were all grown up and out on their own now, so the constant drain on his finances had just about ceased. He hadn't actually seen or heard too much from them over the rest of his army years. His ex had apparently talked abundantly to the children about his many shortcomings, making them rather unwilling to spend any time with him. They hadn't proved so bashful lately, though, especially when they were in trouble or needed money urgently. He grimaced ruefully at that thought. Oh well, he hadn't actually been around much for them when they were younger, so he supposed it was the least he could do.

Marriage certainly hadn't exactly proved very fortuitous for him at all, that was for bloody sure. Maybe he was allergic to it. He'd actually had second go at it, with a British school-teacher he'd met during a two-year stint in Singapore with the battalion. But it turned out to be nothing more than a flight of fancy, born of isolation in the tropics and the bountiful overseas allowances for married couples. The marriage was on the rocks almost before the honeymoon was over. She was 10 years younger than him and had romantic ideas and career aspirations for him. But he was already too set in his ways to change his habits much.

She was forever taking tea with the officers' ladies and demanding to know why he couldn't take a commission, when all he wanted to do when he wasn't in the jungle was drink with his mates in the sergeants' mess and warrant officers' mess. It was two different cultures and never the twain shall meet. Once the initial lust was over, they found they had nothing really in common and were divorced just over a year later, although he'd got out of that one lightly enough because they hadn't been together long enough to have accumulated much. From then on, in the rather crude words of one of his thrice-divorced fellow soldiers, he didn't want to own one any more but maybe just borrow it once in a while.

No one seemed to have any great regard for an old soldier, either. Vietnam hadn't been a popular war and the politicians didn't want to know the veterans. It seemed they were just an embarrassment to the Government which, in pandering to the peaceniks and in trying to balance the books, had rapidly undermined the armed forces by steadily cutting the defence budget to the bone.

Ray knew that a lot of his old comrades or their families who had been affected in some way, mentally or physically, by their service were finding it very hard to get any sort of recognition or assistance for these problems, despite the RSA lobbying hard on their behalf. It seemed that the Government agencies, whose job it was to look after these sorts of people, were better trained in how to avoid assisting them rather than how to help them. He sympathised with those battling for support and reflected on how lucky he'd been. His children were all hale and hearty and he didn't have any major health problems.

Upon finally taking his own discharge, Ray had found his army service and experience, which included leadership and instructional courses along with years of practical use and knowledge, counted for absolutely nothing with potential employers. They just weren't recognised. You had to have a bit of paper that said you had a university degree or something similar before they'd even have considered you for any sort of a managerial role. He quickly learned from sad experience that most of the young whiz-kids with degrees who were put into management roles lacked practical experience and were almost entirely deficit of man-management ability. They obviously didn't teach that skill in the bloody universities, that was for sure.

In the infantry at least, inexperienced officers straight out of officer school were put with an old experienced sergeants to teach them the ropes. Of course, some thought they already knew it all because they were officers born to lead men, but generally these ones were pretty quickly put into their place. Ray could still remember one stuck-up officer telling his troops he was an officer because he was born different. He wasn't too amused when one of his soldiers asked him if that meant he sat down to piss. The whole platoon had cracked up and the embarrassed officer threatened to charge the cheeky private. But out of the army, Ray had met frustration after frustration in his efforts to find suitable and satisfying work without being messed around. His lucky break came finally when he met his old mate Blue at a battalion reunion. This meeting led to big changes and was responsible him getting the job he now had.

Blue had never bothered to get married – probably a wise move in retrospect. He was a tall, thin wiry bloke, some five years older than Ray, and he had also always been a rank or two ahead of him. While the two had never actually served in the same company, they'd become quite firm friends over the years, mainly through their mutual interest in running. Blue had always been a mad keen marathon runner and although Ray's athletic appetite didn't quite extend to running that far and 10 miles was his preferred lot, they had done quite a bit of training together, especially after his first divorce when both had lived in the barracks.

Blue took his discharge a few years ahead of Ray and headed straight to Perth, where he had an ex-Aussie SAS contact and gone into the cash-in-transit armed security business as an armed guard. It was quite a well-paid job, especially compared to New Zealand pay rates. You were generally your own boss once out on the road and a lot of the guys had some sort of military or police background anyway. So, with some exceptions, they were not out-and-out dickheads like so many of the civvies he had worked with in his previous jobs.

At the reunion, Blue saw his old mate was totally bored and at a very loose end. He talked him into visiting Perth, then cunningly introduced him to the state manager of the security company, an ex Aussie air force man. The guy had assured Ray that with his background, he'd definitely be welcomed on board once he'd shifted over and done the necessary courses. It wasn't a difficult decision for Ray. He was flat-arse bored in New Zealand anyway and Blue had offered to put him up in Perth until he got on his feet. The money was better, there were plenty of Kiwis over there, and the climate was better. Blue reckoned he wore a T-shirt virtually all year round because they didn't really have that much of a winter to speak of. So he quickly sold up or gave away most of his few possessions, jumped on to the big bird and away he went.

Once in Perth, he flew through a police check and several security-related courses, including one to qualify for the company-issued weapon, the Smith & Wesson .38 revolver. Although he had never actually fired this particular weapon during his time in the army, he'd fired thousands of rounds with a 9mm Browning and had taught many students to fire it also. So handguns weren't exactly new to him. In fact, it was virtually the same calibre as the Browning and he soon found it was not only a lot easier and safer to handle, but it seemed to pack more grunt as well.

In the army, Ray had been taught, and in turn instructed his own students, in the rapid alignment method of firing a handgun. In the never-to-be-forgotten words of his instructor, "in battle the handgun is generally a close-quarter back-up weapon to your main fire power. If you really need to use it because of a stoppage to your main fire power, you probably won't have time for any fancy aiming because the enemy will more than likely be right in your face and you'll need to do something to discourage him real quickly".

Rapid alignment involved looking over the top of the foresight with both eyes open and firing the weapon into the centre of the mass of the target. Generally double taps (firing two rounds one after another) were used for greater impact. With both eyes, you had the advantage of peripheral vision, being more aware of what was going on around you and where the next possible danger was coming from. Again, in the words of the instructor: "It'll soon make him forget his original intention was to take you out when he's busy trying to digest the couple of rounds you've put into his gut."

It had taken much practice, a fair few thousand rounds and the realisation that firing a pistol accurately wasn't quite as easy as it looked before he had become proficient. The secret was good hand-eye co-ordination, a good grip and a cool head. Once he'd mastered this, it was a skill never to be forgotten. After even more practice, he found he was almost as good firing without raising the weapon to eye level at all. He had the ability to place his rounds accurately into whatever ever he was firing at from any stance – a possibly life-saving advantage at close quarters.

His army students had always been amazed at how he could

just pick up any pistol and almost nonchalantly place his rounds instinctively and swiftly into a tight group at the centre of the target, without even appearing to aim. Of course, he always reminded them, the targets weren't firing back. But he always stressed that an ability to fire instinctively and accurately at close quarters was a great advantage in a tight corner. It could well, he always told them, save their own or someone else's lives.

He'd never actually had recourse to fire a handgun in anger during his army career, although a fair few magazines of 7.62 SLR rounds had disappeared out the barrel of his rifle at some very frantic and scary times on active service. The upshot of all his experience was when it came time to qualify with the Smith & Wesson, he took to it quickly, even though he hadn't fired any sort of a weapon at all for some few years. The weapon may have differed from what he was used to, but the basics remained the same.

His instructors were suitably impressed, some even openly envious at his dexterity, speed and accuracy with the weapon. Some of the younger blokes on the course had started out by dismissing him as too old for the game and foolishly boasted about how good they were with a handgun. They were made to feel rather stupid when they saw the way the guts were ripped out of his target. "The weapon doesn't know how old the finger is that squeezes the titty, sonny," Ray had said to one of the more strident oldie-knockers at the time.

All candidates for employment also had to be thoroughly familiarised with the State laws governing the carriage and use of weapons while on bona fide cash-in-transit duties. Great emphasis was placed in explaining the term "vicarious liability", described as the joint responsibility of both employer and employee when the weapon was used outside the guidelines laid down by State law.

Ray felt the company was almost paranoid about this. It was constantly rammed down their throats on a daily basis during the initial training. They seemed more worried that the guards might use their weapons, perhaps hitting an innocent bystander, and the repercussions from that, than the actual loss of what they were carrying.

In fact the company's advice was to comply with any request by would-be robbers and surrender the money. Ray's neck hair had bristled on hearing this, but he was smart enough to realise he was a new boy on the block and shouldn't cause waves. Not at that stage, anyway. But he resolved to talk to Blue about it later. The training, with a fair bit of boring classroom time included, was over soon enough and he began work initially as the escort in a three-man crew on a casual basis. After completing the 90-day probation period, during which he learned a hell of a lot more about the job he was employed full-time by the company SAFE AS (Safe and Secure) as a fully-fledged cash-in-transit armed guard.

The job involved going round businesses and banks, dropping off their ordered money or picking up takings for delivery back to base where it would be counted, banked or delivered on their behalf. A big part of the job was delivering change that had been prepared at the company's large, fort-like base. Mondays and Fridays were always especially busy. Then there were special jobs, such as meeting and transporting shipments of gold, silver, gems or any other valuable items, and securing and transporting money to and from big events.

You didn't need to be a brain surgeon to do the work, but apart from being alert at all times, you also had to have a bit of a head for figures because sometimes you actually had to count the money you collected, then issue a receipt. Another very important attribute was people skills – being able to speak to and deal with people from all walks of life, each with their own worries and anxieties.

SAFE AS was one of the largest security companies in town, with about 80 permanent staff, a large number of casuals and about 50 vehicles of various shapes and sizes, most of them armoured and alarmed and exceedingly difficult to break into. Probably at least a third of the employees were guys like Ray and Blue, in their 50s or early 60s, with careers in the armed forces or police behind them. The rest were younger – in their late 20s, 30s or 40s – and of some them also had a few years' service in the military or police behind them.

While generally they all got on well together, a few of the younger blokes resented working under the older, generally more reliable and well-respected veterans. A few really struggled to hide their irritation, maintaining that the old codgers were past it and wouldn't know what to do or be quick enough if something did go down. Old Blue was probably one of the fittest there anyway and was still running the odd marathon. He'd just laugh and reply to the 'Dad's army' jibes with: "Listen mate, I was in uniform when you were in liquid form." This usually made the others laugh and put the taunter in his place, although not gracefully at times.

Ray copied Blue when he struck the same scenario and would always ask if the younger guy knew the story of the young bull and the old bull. If an answer was not forthcoming, one of the other older guys would always say that he hadn't, just to ensure the story could be told. Away Ray would go: A farmer pushed a young bull and an old bull into a paddock of cows and left them there. The young bull saw the cows and bellowed: "Look! Cows! Let's run over and fuck one." The old bull snorted quietly: "Nah, we'll walk over and fuck the lot." This joke always produced a laugh from the oldies even though they'd heard it a dozen times before, while the victim sometimes simmered a touch, suspecting that perhaps he was being patronised somehow. One young bloke even reckoned that if life was a game of cards then Ray and Blue would just be a pair of old cunts, which of course got all the younger ones laughing. But generally, the camaraderie was not unlike being back in the army. Sort of.

Ray soon discovered that old Blue, who hadn't had much to do with handguns before, wasn't even was half as good a shot with the pistol as he was. This was the subject of much good-natured bantering between the two. When Ray had seen the size of Blue's group at the six-monthly qualifying shoot, he'd laughed and suggested that perhaps Blue might have been better off with a claymore – an anti-personnel mine packed with ball-bearings, an ideal and deadly ambush weapon especially when deployed en masse. An effective "area weapon", in army parlance. Blue took this suggestion as a mortal insult and bristled every time Ray called him 'the claymore man' when conversation turned to marksmanship.

Two years fairly flew by and Ray had settled in well to Australia and to the job. He nearly always found himself appointed crew leader in charge of two or three others. Unfortunately this meant he hardly ever worked with Blue, who was generally rostered as a crew leader as well. Three-man crews were generally sent into busier parts of town, where larger amounts of money were collected and carried and finding suitable parking was a problem.

The job was always interesting with a lot of variety, which included going country on occasion. It suited Ray's restless spirit, but always at the back of the mind the realization that today might be the day someone might choose to have a go at them. As one of the ex-Aussie army guys put it: "Today might be the day the teddy bears have their picnic."

The armoured trucks were virtually invulnerable to normal attack. It would take simply too much time for criminals to neutralize the outside guards, smash their way into the truck then take out the driver (who in all probability would have driven off by then anyway). Then they would have to get the money from the drop safe inside the vehicle itself which could only be accessed with a key back at base. Driving off with the vehicle was not an option, either, as they were all equipped with sat nav locators which could be set off either by the crew or automatically on an illegal entry, which also shut the vehicle down after a few minutes anyway.

No, the most likely way an attempted robbery would take place was when the guards were walking back from a business to the vehicle with money in hand. The takings from some of the larger companies quite often amounted to a princely amount and would make quite a reward for those prepared to take a risk. At times and especially in the city, the guards were forced to park the vehicle a fair way from some of the collection points. So they had a long walk back, with sometimes hundreds of thousands of dollars in hand. This was when they were the most vulnerable and would be the ideal and most logical time for anyone to make a grab. Ray and Blue were both exceptionally vigilant in these circumstances, keeping their eyes peeled for anything suspicious and sizing up any ideal ambush points. They both reckoned that some, although not all, of their co-workers were a bit blasé about the danger at times, no doubt thinking it would never happen because it never had so far in their fair city.

There were actually some directives concerning attempted robberies from management that both of them thought were pretty ridiculous The first was the instruction that the guards immediately surrender and hand over the money and their weapons if surprised and ordered to by armed robbers while walking from a premises back to the vehicle. The second was the insistence the vehicle leave the scene immediately if there were an attempted robbery of the outside guards, ostensibly taking away any reason for the criminals to try and use them as hostages to gain access. The management reasoned that the guards were less likely to be shot following these procedures, but the two ex-soldiers were a little bit sceptical about this theory, especially given the type of people desperate enough to attempt such a crime. Ray and Blue both thought the typical robber would have had no formal weapons training, be full of adrenaline and drugs or alcohol and would not give a fuck about taking a life or, being incompetent, would open fire without meaning to.

Neither Ray nor Blue wanted any part of a surrender scenario and both avowed that they would rather take their chances in defending themselves. As Ray said indignantly to Blue: "I'm not surrendering to no bastard. They'll probably fucking shoot us anyway. I'd rather take my chances on their not being too crash hot with their weapons and have a bloody go." Bugging out in the truck while your mates were being held up also went totally against the grain as well. 'Never leave a mate behind' was the army motto, and they couldn't see any reason to change that. They also reckoned that once one lot meekly surrendered the money, it would only encourage more crims to have a go and then it would probably become open slather on all armed guards. However, both men were wise enough to keep these opinions to themselves, in the interest of keeping their jobs and in the hope that they'd never be called upon to make such a decision.

Generally, the job was well-paid and enjoyable. Occasionally they got a three-day weekend and as well as running, the two friends also discovered the joys of golf and in particular the 19th hole. If life was indeed a game of cards, it was certainly dealing kindly to this pair of old cunts at present.

Saint Patrick's Day was invariably a huge one in Perth. Anybody who was Irish, of Irish descent or even knew a bad Irish joke seemed to want to celebrate it by getting as inebriated as possible. As an Irish mate of Blue's had once commented, on Saint Patrick's day there's only two sorts of people – the Irish and the wannabe Irish. There were half a dozen or more Irish pubs scattered around the city. With Irish bands and dancers entertaining, they did a huge trade on 17 March, while many other bars also adopted an Irish theme for the day. All in all it was usually a highly celebrated and well-lubricated occasion with many a gallon of Guinness and Kilkenny poured, a fair few bottles of Jamesons or Bushmills breached and the cause of many a hangover the following morning

This year was to prove no different. In fact, it was probably going be more celebrated than normal, given that it fell on a Friday with a whole weekend to get over it. Absenteeism was rife and bosses everywhere pulled their hair out in frustration. SAFE AS found itself as affected as a lot of other firms on the day, with a record number of late book-offs. A variety of excuses was offered but generally the absence related to a desire to suitably celebrate the occasion. Casuals were frantically phoned but an abnormal number weren't even contactable, being already out on the town. Those who could be contacted were heading out and didn't want to work. Run schedules were quickly altered and crews were hastily swapped about as dispatchers frantically tried to juggle things so the firm could fulfil its commitments. Ray had supposed to have been leading a three-man crew on the CBD run but found himself minus both a driver and an escort. After some frantic swapping and reshuffling, a robbing-Peter-to-pay-Paul operation, Ray was delighted to learn that Blue had been drafted as his driver, while the escort was to be one of the biggest critics of "the old dicks". It was all shaping up to be an extra-interesting day.

They set sail for the city nearly an hour late, saddled with a host of last-minute add-on jobs because a couple of runs had to be canned because of the lack of staff. Then they got caught up in even worse traffic than usual, which with Murphy's Law to the fore and especially on Saint Pat's Day, which was much busier than usual. The city was fair humming by the time they eventually got there. There'd been many early breakfasts various hostelries and a lot of the partakers were already well on the way, drinking with great gusto, enjoying the music and the singing and dancing of the Celtic bands and Colleens. There was a lot more foot traffic than usual, parking was already at a premium and snarl-ups and frustration were the order of the morning. City officials were busy closing some lanes on the streets surrounding the square by the time they arrived, readying for the St. Patrick's Day parade through the mall at lunchtime.

The SAFE AS boys quickly felt the backwash of the celebrations because even though they were running late themselves, several businesses still weren't ready for them because staff hadn't turned up or they were just too busy. They'd usually be asked to return later for the pick-up in this scenario, which was a bit of a pain in the butt and threatened to turn the already over-large and behind-schedule run into a marathon.

By the time the parade started at noon, they weren't even a third of the way through the run, and traffic was virtually at a standstill. The mass of people on the footpaths also made it almost impossible to move safely with money on foot and so, not without feeling some frustration, they decided they might as well break for lunch and watch the spectacle themselves.

The parade was a totally hilarious, the kind of uncoordinated shambles that only the Irish could disorganise. The skirl of the pipes and thumping of the drums not only attracted the shoppers and employees from their work places but also the patrons from the bars. Many, of course, had been drinking steadily since breakfast time and were already three sheets to the wind. And with a wee drop of the craythur helping to settle inhibitions, some of the more merry watchers just couldn't resist the temptation to join in. Once one started, others followed suit, soon creating a mass of inebriated unofficial participants staggering along with the parade, performing their own interpretations of Irish singing and dancing.

They wove in and out of the ranks of the bands, singing loudly, usually some sort of beer or spirit in hand and threatening to turn the whole parade into one giant cluster fuck. It was all good-natured and entertaining stuff, though, producing plenty of belly laughs and the police stood back benignly with the rest of the on-lookers also enjoying the unruly spectacle. They did make a move, however, when, much to the amusement of the crowd, an intoxicated woman, all dressed in green and sporting green hair also, started lifting up the kilts of the bandsmen to find out what was beneath. To their credit and the amusement of the crowd, the bandsmen didn't turn a hair, or anything else, but just kept playing while she made her detailed examination. Mad Mary, as she was apparently named, was quickly escorted back to the footpath amid the clapping and cheering of the crowd. It was more for her own safety than anything else, although she did give the police more than an ear full in a thick Irish brogue after she was set free. The police didn't really give a toss, though. They were obviously as determined as the rest of the crowd were to enjoy the day and, not really wanting to arrest anyone, they just ignored her.

All in all it was a thoroughly entertaining hour enjoyed by everyone, including the SAFE AS boys. And they didn't forget to relieve Blue, who as the driver would spend most of the day in the truck. Delightful as the parade had been, they were now even more behind schedule. Once the crowd dwindled, the truck set off and the crew tried to make up for lost time. The rest of the afternoon flashed by as if in a blur. In and out of businesses, delivering change coming out with the takings, collecting banking that in several instances which had to be delivered before 4.30pm. Some bars were also on the agenda and most were still full of half-tanked happy patrons, a few offering to buy them a beer. Several women kissed them or rather slobbered on them. The funniest occasion was when the escort Dave, to his horror, was hugged and kissed by a big, ugly, elderly half-pissed Irishman "Fuckin' old dick," snarled Dave as he wiped the slobber off his face.

They fielded many calls from base: Customer inquiry. When were they going to be here? When were they going to be there? Could you do this first? Could you do that soon? It was most frustrating because they were already running late and certainly didn't need any interference.

Ray kept his cool and told base that because of the circumstances and the lateness, he wasn't going to divert from the original plan. This wasn't accepted really well back at base, where they had no idea what conditions were like. As they used to say in the army, flexibility might be the keynote, but the last thing the sharp end boys needed when the shit was flying around their ears was the base wallah telling them what to do.

The crew finally got around to doing the job at the home base of Macefield's, one of the biggest department stores in WA, nearly three hours beyond this customer's preferred time. There were still three petrol stations to do after that, but they stayed open 24 hours a day and Ray had deliberately left them until last, despite protestations from base. The sun was sinking and the shadows rapidly encroaching on the daylight as they made their way down the narrow one-way service lane that meandered round behind the back of Macefield's and several other retailers. There wasn't too much room to negotiate, just turn-offs into each store's loading and unloading docks. "Not even enough room to swing a dead cat," Blue had observed once. "Or a willing ewe," he added immediately, with a nod to Aussie piss-taking about Kiwi "sheep-shaggers".

To gain entrance to Macefield's, the crew had to ring the bell at a fire exit on the side of the building. The one-way system prevented the truck from parking directly outside, otherwise other vehicles wouldn't be able to get past. Instead, they had to park at a slight bend about 30 metres further back. Pulling right over against the wall and parking over a narrow walking path, the driver could still see the entrance and there was just enough room for another truck to squeeze by. Neither Blue nor Ray liked this arrangement very much because it wasn't tactically sound - too far to walk and too much time for someone to have a go at them. It was a perfect spot for an ambush, with nowhere for the truck to go except backwards if the service lane was blocked off. The truck was a sitting duck. When they mentioned this at work, the hierarchy had agreed but said it was the best of several poor options. There was no parking to be had close to the front of the store, either – it was right on one of the busiest streets in Perth.

Ray and the escort Dave set off up the alley pushing the trolley heavily laden with the change the store had been crying out for all afternoon, while Blue settled down patiently to wait, as he had been doing all day. He watched them arrive safely at the door, ring the bell, wait for a few minutes then disappear inside. He always kept his wits about him when employed as a driver, continually looking around all over the place. Old habits die hard and even though he couldn't see too much through the mirrors behind him, parked as he was right on a bend, he still looked. He also kept glancing up the lane toward the entrance from the main road, about 60 metres away.

After a few minutes, he noticed a darkly clothed, youngish-looking guy, with what looked like a beanie pulled down low to just above his eyes, walking past the entrance to the road. Unlike all the rest of the passers-by, however, this guy stopped and looked deliberately towards the truck, eyeballing it for nearly a full minute before continuing on out of sight. Slightly suspicious, thought Blue as he muttered: "Nosy bastard."

The time dragged by ever so slowly. If it had been a frustrating day for the crew leader and escort, it had been even worse for him, stuck in the truck most of the time. Almost 10 more minutes elapsed before he noticed what looked remarkably like the same young chap, leaning round the corner this time and looking down toward him again. Blue's interest was definitely now aroused. Just as he was just considering radioing Ray, two things happened.

The side-entrance door opened Ray and Dave stepped back into the lane and began to walk towards him, Dave pushing the empty change trolley and Ray in front with the money bag under his arm. At the same time, what looked like a big red Ford Falcon suddenly framed the exit to the service lane, nose pointing menacingly down toward them. Blue's scalp tingled. "Something's on here," he thought, leaning on the horn with his elbow and reaching for the radio at the same time. Ray and Dave turned about quickly about as, with a screech of rubber on bitumen, the car accelerated down the lane towards them. They weren't coming to say a friendly "Gidday mate," that was for sure.

Ray's pistol almost magically filled his hand as the vehicle bore swiftly down on them. Instinctively he ducked down, yelling "take cover" to Dave, who still holding the trolley with one hand while making a rather belated and clumsy grab for his weapon. But in that stark confined space there was nowhere to take cover. There was absolutely nowhere to hide.

An evil-looking long black cylindrical object suddenly protruded out of the empty back window on the driver's side of the red Falcon. "Look out, the bastards have got a shotgun!" Ray yelled to Dave. As if that wasn't enough to worry about, the front passenger's door then opened as well, and a figure loomed up over the top of the roof holding a handgun in one hand. BOOM! BOOM! The shotgun report reverberated down the narrow confines of the service lane. Ray staggered as he felt a sudden gouging on the right side of his head something tugging at his shirt and then the sharp painful stinging in his head, right arm and ear. But he had only been on the outer of the spread of shot, and it was Dave who had borne the brunt of it. Collapsing heavily onto his back, he screamed loudly, blood pooling quickly over his stomach then oozing down on to the road.

Ray, momentarily stunned by his own wound, was shocked and

frightened to see his partner blown off his feet like that. But ingrained years of discipline and experience quickly re-asserted themselves. Instinctively, he went into a battle crouch, thinking almost detachedly: "Well, so much for fucking surrendering, then." As the shotgun thankfully withdrew back inside the car, he let rip. BANG! BANG! A double tap and the windscreen of the car shattered. A slight hesitation and a shift of target, then BANG! BANG! The front right tyre of the rapidly slowing vehicle blew out, causing it to skew heavily to the right, the front guard smashing into the brick wall. The vehicle stopped dead and the driver was totally out of sight.

Ray sank down on to one knee as he got off another wild double tap at the figure on the passenger's side who, having recovered from the crash, was steadily firing at him again. Fortunately, he was still firing one-handed and not very accurately – not yet, anyway. Ray's weapon was empty. He needed to reload quickly as rounds hissed angrily past his ear ricocheting viciously off the wall then whining back perilously close as he was showered with stinging chips and brick dust. Some sort of powerful hand gun, he thought; hard to control at the best of times, and especially with one hand. Luckily for Ray's sake, the gunman was piss-useless with it, spraying his rounds all over the fucking place. Ray remembered later on also thinking, must have a fucking big magazine on that bastard.

Blue hit the alarm button as the firing reverberated loudly down the service lane then savagely accelerated the truck toward the scene of the conflict. He saw Ray bend and pick up Dave's unfired weapon off the ground where it had fallen, then go back into the crouch. "Good thinking, horse," he thought.

There was still no driver to be seen in the front seat of the car, but the extremely dangerous, evil-looking long cylindrical object suddenly poked over the top of now-open back door. It had obviously been reloaded and the holder was now out of the car, standing and lining up for another shot, having been hampered and slowed by the length of the weapon in the confines of the car.

His upper midriff stood out almost like a target silhouetted behind the window frame.

Ray steadied, suddenly noticing the pistol man wasn't firing at him anymore. Hopefully he'd had a stoppage or was reloading or something. He'd certainly fired enough fucking rounds. But he had to nail the bastard with the shotgun before he fired again. That weapon was fucking dangerous at close quarters. It could rip a man apart. This awful fear motivated his determination.

It wasn't a hard shot for a man with his experience, especially this close. If it hadn't been for the circumstances, he would have likened it to shooting ducks in a barrel. BANG! BANG! BANG! BANG! Two double taps slammed through the vacant window frame, right into the breadbasket. The figure was propelled rapidly backwards then sank down out of sight, shotgun clattering to the ground. Thank fuck for that, the murderous shotgun was out of the play.

Ray threw his last two rounds wildly at the pistol man, who had suddenly erupted back into business again, then went to ground. "What the fuck do I do now?" he thought desperately as he emptied the chamber of Dave's weapon and fumbled for a speed loader

Meanwhile, the pistol shooter was right out of the car, leaning over the front of the passenger's door, now with both hands on the weapon and taking deliberate aim. Ray was frantically reloading and bracing himself to be hit when suddenly the truck crashed on to the scene. It smashed into the car door with a solid crump, snapping it back against the pistol shooter's body and pinning him upright between door and car. The continuing momentum then drove the whole length of the car solidly against the wall with a final and resounding crash.

Blue cut the engine and jumped out, weapon in hand. There was a sudden silence after all the firing and noise. It was almost an anti-climax.

"You right, Ray?" yelled Blue, as screaming suddenly started. The pistol man was obviously not much appreciating his present position in life.

"I think so," answered Ray, now with the reloaded weapon. "Jesus, you old bastard, you certainly fixed him up with that truck."

"Fuck, he asked for it," was Blue's retort. "He fuckin' did and all. Look I'll cover, and you check the driver and that other bastard. Get their weapons, but be fuckin' careful."

"Right," said Blue. Army post-contact procedures automatically took over as in the distance, sirens began to wail. They quickly found they couldn't get into the car because of the truck being jammed against it, so Blue had to get in and back it off. Ray then saw the handgun lying on the ground and toed it carefully well away from its user, not that he was that much interested in it anymore by then. The pistol man still remained upright pinned by the crushed door, screaming now tapered off to loud but constant moaning.

Ray, swaying a bit now and dripping blood from right arm, head and torn ear, covered as Blue forced the door open, releasing the trapped gunman who screeched as he collapsed on to the ground then continued doing so as he was unceremoniously dragged clear of the vehicle. Blue then found the driver slumped down across the front seat groaning quietly to himself, a sawn off .22 on the seat next to him. His face was a mess of blood and lacerations, eyes swollen and tightly closed, injured by the flying glass from the shattered windscreen.

Blue gingerly picked up and placed the .22 well out of harm's way before pulling the driver roughly out of the vehicle by the shirt and letting him fall heavily onto the ground. He then dragged him roughly over to where Ray was guarding his companion. They didn't worry too much about the shotgun man. Ray knew he'd nailed him good. He was obviously beyond pain, making no noise at all. They couldn't move the car, crumpled as it was, and the body and the weapon were somewhere beneath it all. So they just left things as they were. Both the wounded would-be robbers were moaning and groaning constantly, all fight gone out of them. They had bitten the bullet and come off second best but the two old soldiers weren't taking any chances of an encore.

They stood, side by side, both far more shaken by the sudden violence than they'd ever admit to, covering the area with weapons at the ready. A few passers-by who'd heard the firing began timorously approaching the scene, shocked looks on their faces, it was all over bar the mopping up. Ray suddenly sagged at the knees and plonked down heavily on to his arse, wiping the blood from the side of his face. The shock of the violent action and his own injuries had finally caught up to him.

Blue was suddenly concerned about his mate quickly went to him. Ray, annoyed at his sudden weakness, said testily: "I'm okay,

I'm okay. Look, better check Dave out. He's bloody worse than I am."

Blue was bent over Dave, who was badly wounded, riddled with pellets but still alive, when a white car nosed into the entrance to the service lane and stopped as what looked like the sole occupant gazed down upon the scene. "Fuck me, not more of them," said Blue. Ray dragged himself painfully to his feet, instinctively checking the load of his weapon again. But they needn't have bothered. Whoever it was, possibly the getaway driver, obviously didn't want any part of the drama and, with a squeal of burning rubber, he reversed speedily and booted noisily away, leaving tyre marks imprinted on the bitumen.

Dave was holding on to his stomach with his face set in an awful grimace as he tried not to scream. "Hang on there, Dave," said Blue. "Help's on its way." Dave waved an arm in reply, signalling Blue to lean down. "You pair of old cunts," he rasped. "You fuckin' win."

The two old soldiers stood side by side, guarding the scene, waiting for the police, sirens wailing ever closer. If life was indeed a game of cards, then a pair of old soldiers had certainly won this hand. Ray, light-headed with shock and fatigue, laughed to himself that he would never again complain about the boredom of life on Civvy Street.

"Hey, Blue," he said suddenly with a bit of a giggle.

"What?" replied Blue, surprised that he could find any humour in the situation.

"I told you you'd be better off with an area weapon," Ray said, indicating the truck.

Blue's retort was unrepeatable.

AN OLD DOG FOR A HARD ROAD

Jock was out for his morning walk, talking to himself as usual and doing particularly well at both pursuits. Passers-by, on seeing his lips moving, generally gave him a wide berth, thinking perhaps he might be slightly touched. To be honest, there wasn't that much of him to put the frighteners on anyone, really. Still, he was in pretty good nick for a rising 70-year-old. With an extremely active brain that had energized his wiry body all his life, he still had great muscle tone and, as a few people had found out recently to their cost, his fitness and agility belied his age and size.

Growing up in one of the poorer areas of Glasgow and serving 25 years in the NZ Army, including active service in a couple of conflicts, meant he was no stranger to violence and could well care of himself. He'd been down a hard road in his younger days. Not being very big, he'd had had to learn to be evasive. Over the years, he'd learned many little tricks he could use to cut an oversized aggressor down quickly and efficiently. Some of his younger victims, who'd overestimated themselves and underestimated Jock's ability, were astounded when bested by this little old stroppy Scottish prick.

As a youth, Jock was a boxer and gained a reasonably high level in the lighter weight divisions. The army was quick to identify and utilise this skill, having Jock give young soldiers lessons. Many a large young man had gone up against him thinking he was easy meat; nearly as many had become frustrated then angry on discovering that not only could they not hit him, but he packed a mean old wallop himself. His trademark blow was a sort of a flicked whiplash jab, generally delivered flush on to the nose. It made many an eye water and temper fray, especially when the victim's mates laughed. Some would actually lose it completely and start throwing huge round-house bombs at him. But old Jock simply wouldn't be there when they arrived. He'd either be well back out of range or around to one side, giving his enraged assailant a cuff around the earhole.

While Old Jock generally never went looking for trouble, he wasn't one to back away either. He was very quick to go on the offensive if he or friends were threatened. Rule No 1 for him was the old infantryman's adage: The best means of defence is attack. And when Jock attacked, he did it ruthlessly and quickly. Rule No 2 for Jock was "ambush is always the best option". He generally never bothered with a warning, or blethering as he put it, but just got stuck straight in. And his final rule, especially given his age now, was: "A weapon is always better than no weapon." He'd demonstrated this recently when he'd used a spade to great effect on a couple of the young thugs who'd tried to break into Mac and Tracy's place over the road. Of course, the girl and dog had helped out too, and the thieves had probably been more scared of Blade than him, although they'd told the police "that Scotsman was fuckin' mad."

He'd received a bit of a verbal warning on the level of violence he'd used that day. But as he'd said to the policeman, "did ya want me to let them rape the lassie, then?" There'd been no answer to that, of course.

Tracy and Mac's father, who'd served with Jock and fought a war alongside him, was extremely grateful that Jock had been around when the break-in occurred. Tracy had been crook and at home on her own. He couldn't thank him enough, but Jock had just shrugged it off saying: "Och, it was nothing. The girl and the dog woulda probably beaten them on they own anyway. They were a fookin' bunch of pansies."

Actually that particular bunch of pansies was the subject of Jock's conversation with himself today. In his opinion, they'd had got off far too lightly – especially the one who'd grabbed the lassie, bruising her and threatening to rape her. He'd ended up in hospital under observation for 10 days supposedly suffering from concussion, but very probably had milked it to the max. When he had finally gone up to court, his lawyer made a real meal of "the level of violence committed upon him", the puir wee lad's injuries and, of course, the bullshit wouldn't be complete without his "deprived fatherless background" being trotted out.

Jock had come from a harsh background himself and had no time for that sort of crap.

"Fookin' rubbish," Jock said to himself as he walked along. In his opinion, they'd all got off far too lightly. The would-be rapist copped only six months, which he'd probably serve half of before getting out, and the rest received only supervision. "They're too fookin' soft these fookin' days."

One of them even had the cheek to threaten him. "We'll get you, you old cunt," he'd said on encountering Jock in the courthouse dunny before the case was called. "Will ye nae come back and we'll do it all again then?" Jock had answered with a smile and raised quizzical eyebrows, borrowing the advertising jingle for his favourite Scotch but knowing the guy wouldn't start anything in the courthouse and probably wasn't game on his own anyway. And he wasn't. "You're fuckin' mad, you old bugger," he'd replied, backing hurriedly away toward the door. "Aye, and you're a fookin' parasitic scumbag thief, and I'll see you when you come back laddie. If you're fookin' game, that is," Jock replied.

He'd be keeping his eyes open just in case, though he wasn't worried about himself so much but for Millie, and more especially if they did come and find her at home alone. The rest probably wouldn't be game to start anything by themselves but, with the rapist appearing to be the leader due out any time now from the ridiculously light sentence he'd got, that could change, so he'd better stick close to home. He had himself an equalizer on hand, a big staff, ostensibly a walking aid but long enough and thick enough to make an awesome weapon when applied in the right manner.

"Och, bring it on laddies," Jock said to himself and smiled, causing an approaching lady to swerve and circle warily around him.

"I think he likes you now, Jock," Mac said "Have you noticed that ever since you and he dished up those wankers, he thinks you're a fellow combatant now."

Jock laughed. "Aye, he probably does. But do ye reckon he'd let me take him for a walk and stay with me if I let him go?" he asked.

"I reckon he might, but we better have a couple of dry runs first just to make sure. You take him for a walk, then let him go in the park, and if he'll come back to you instead of coming home on his own, that might just about cure all the problems while I'm away."

Mac's dog Blade had become even more notorious with the Council rangers after all the publicity in the local press about him, Tracy and Jock comprehensively routing the four would-be burglars.

Already in the bad books with the dog rangers for continually getting out of the backyard, wandering and being uncatchable, his reputation had grown even more after that incident. Mac had had a warning about him attacking people as well, even though the only people he'd attacked had been breaking into his house.

The mother of one of the pansies had even called for Blade to be put down because of the wounds inflicted on various legs and arses. The police themselves had squashed that call, however, by pointing out that while they didn't condone a dog attacking people, it had probably stopped several crimes being committed and if the perpetrators hadn't tried to break in, they wouldn't have been bitten. Which was hopefully true. He hadn't bitten anyone outside their property, as far as Mac knew, but they'd have to watch him carefully because he was a bit of a canine celebrity now. But if Blade would let Jock take him for a daily walk while Mac was away, that could fix everything, and Jock was willing. He walked every day anyway come hail or shine and for bloody miles. Accompanying him might just about satisfy Blade's wanderlust and perhaps be an answer to a prayer.

So they planned it all out. Mac pretended he was going out but just went over to Jock's for half an hour. Then the two of them went back and while Mac snuck in the front door, Jock went in the back gate called the dog and grabbed the leash from where it hung in the back porch. Looking through the bedroom window, Mac saw Blade go willingly enough to Jock and, knowing that he was going for a walk, let himself be leashed up. Away the two went. Phase one successful.

Jock then took Blade for a long walk, finally ending up at the park where he let him off the leash. Blade took off and had a good run around in the trees, looking for real or imaginary enemies. He had a roll or two then did what dogs normally prefer to do when they are away from home, enthusiastically scratched the grass afterwards, which was probably a dog's way of washing its hands, and eventually returned to see what old Jock was up to. He was sitting on a park bench watching and when he put his hand out Blade stuck his nose straight into it and let Jock scratch his ears. After a few minutes of this, Jock got the leash clipped it back on and away home they went. Phase two successful. If Jock did this every day while Mac was away, would this stop the dog's tendency to escape and wander? Phase three yet to be confirmed.

After two more weeks, it was obvious the plan was working like a charm and now Blade would even wait by the gate for Jock to come over early every morning. Tracy reckoned he'd have got the leash down too, if he could have. Soon Jock bought an extendable leash which, attached to his belt, gave Blade more freedom while they were walking and enabled Jock to carry his equalizer, the staff, a lot more comfortably. So while Mac was still definitely his master, Blade accepted Jock as a fill-in and a friend while he was away, and the extremely long walks seemed to curb his instinct to escape and wander on his own. All good.

Beau hadn't liked serving time in the Rangipo Prison farm very much. In fact, he'd hated it. The physical work hadn't suited him at all and he feigned dizzy spells, claiming it was a result of the concussion, to get himself out of some of the more onerous duties. He'd had to put up with a certain amount of taunting, too, once his fellow prisoners learned that he had been bashed into unconsciousness by a sheila. He'd absolutely hated that but had had to eat humble pie, because he'd very quickly learned that there were plenty of much tougher boys than him inside. He'd done only four of the six months before being paroled, but it had been four of the longest months of his life. All his life he had been accustomed to being No 1 but he wasn't even in the top 40 there.

Now he had to live with his mother and was under curfew for the next eight weeks. But that was much better than being inside, and he was back to being No 1. He'd always been able to get around his Mum anyway, and had done so ever since his father died when he was 10. They were left rather well off, not as deprived as the lawyer had claimed, and his mother had spoiled him, giving him almost anything he wanted as he grew up. So he felt the world owed him something

It still rankled him greatly the ragging he'd got in the papers, the court and inside how he and his whole gang were conquered by a girl, a dog and an old man. He'd seen the old prick for the first time at the courthouse, and people had thought his account of the events hilarious. Many had laughed at the fact he'd being beaten unconscious by a sheila, and the old prick had even claimed that the dog and the sheila would probably have been too tough for them on their own, a cause for even more hilarity.

Well, he'd show them. Give it a few weeks or so for the cops to stop looking too closely at him and he'd have a talk to the boys. He wasn't supposed to associate with them under the terms of his parole. But when he could, well then there'd be a certain Scotsman who was going to be paid a visit. Nobody made him a laughing stock and got away with it.

"He's certainly a changed dog, isn't he," Tracy suggested as Jock let Blade off the leash in the back yard a month later. "Aye, lass," came the reply. "I think it's the exercise and the attention he likes. He's like me, he gets bored easy and likes having things to do. He's nae a sit-around hound." Jock had actually been keeping Blade over at his place all day after their morning walks now, off the chain too and quite happy to be there. He only brought him back when Tracy or Mac got home from work, because he was far less likely to roam when someone was around.

"It's good having him here at night when Mac's away. You're a godsend, Jock. Who would have thought you and him would click like that? I always thought he was a one-man dog."

"In a way I think he still is, but I think me and him have the same nature. We cannae keep still for very long."

"Well I'm pleased because I really thought the Council would try and make us get rid of him before, well you know, before those ..."

"Idiots," finished Jock. "Aye, but dinna worry. I don't think you'll see them back here very soon. They were all shite scared of him."

"Still, you be careful Jock. I told Terry one of then threatened you at the courthouse and he said he'd wished you'd told him that then."

"Och, it was nothing. They're full of shite, lass. I don't think they'll be back."

"Just you be careful. You never know with those sort of people."

"Aye lass, nothing to worry about. I'll see you tomorrow."

Jock started to take his leave his leave but then turned back. "By the way, there's a reunion in Palmy in November. Ask your Dad if he's going, next time you're talking to him."

"He probably will. You know him. But I'll ask anyway. Thanks, Jock."

Jock sat on the park seat watching Blade hare off into the large block of native trees being nursed along by conservationists there. He loved it amongst those trees. There were probably no possums because there were always traps set, with absolutely no poison allowed this close to town. Jock didn't quite know what exactly it was Blade found so irresistible in there, but he always made a beeline for them upon being released.

The first few times Jock had let him off the leash, Blade had stayed in there so long he'd been worried he may have gone wandering and went to look for him. But he found him still there running around like a mad egg, chasing down some scent or other, but nothing that Jock could see.

"Aye, you're a wee mad egg alright." Jock shook his head, smiled sat for a while then began musing, casting his mind way, way back to his Glasgow days.

"There he is! I told you the mad old bastard would be somewhere round here! I've seen him walking through here lots of times."

"Great," said Beau. "No one about, too, that's even better. Park up here and we'll sneak up behind the old cunt. We'll see who has the last laugh."

The four thugs bailed out, shut the car doors quietly and began quietly closing the distance between them and Jock. So intent on the past was he that Jock never even heard them till they'd grabbed him, a man on each arm which they brutally twisted up his back.

"Got you, you fucking old cunt!" roared Beau and punched him solidly in the lower abdomen.

Even though completely caught by surprise, Jock still managed to instinctively tighten his stomach muscles which somewhat lessened the blow but he still let out a loud "umph" and sagged as though much worse stricken. "How tough are you now mate!

There's no fuckin' dog to save you!" He gave him another crack in the guts for good measure. This one really hurt and the resultant "umph" was a real one. Jock sagged so heavily on his captors that they let him go suddenly, and he fell to the ground. But he scrambled furiously back to his feet, not wanting to give them the opportunity to use the boot.

"Grab him! Grab him!" screamed Beau, and as one of them attempted to grab his arm again, Jock turned and nutted him, a perfect Liverpool kiss. All of a sudden it was on, the remaining three wrestled him to the ground again and an apoplectic Beau began to administer the boot.

Jock was in real trouble. Once, twice, three times the boot went into his stomach and ribcage area. No one even noticed the nutted and dazed thug slowly picking himself up off the ground and with hand over red gushing nose, stagger back towards the car about 40 metres away. Also in the kerfuffle, no one had noticed the leash lying on the park seat next to the staff.

Jock was on the ground, curled into a ball now and trying to protect himself as best he could from the boots when Blade arrived in nipping good time. Beau had just planted the boot into Jock again when a set of sharp teeth fastened onto his grounded back ankle, held tight and pulled backwards violently.

He screamed and fell back onto his arse, on seeing Blade he frantically wrenched his ankle out of the dog's mouth ripping the skin, scrambled to his feet and set off for the car at the high port. The other pair of heroes had bolted on seeing the dog, so Beau was harassed all the way back, suffering several more bites before reaching the safety of the vehicle and flinging himself into it. He screamed at his mates to get the hell out of there.

With a loud roar, the engine started and with wheels spinning and dust flying everywhere, the four thugs beat a hasty retreat.

Blade then went back to Jock, who was lying on the ground in some pain but laughing his arse off as though he'd never seen anything so funny. It hurt somewhat, but in his mind what he had just witnessed was worth it. Eventually, he pulled himself back up onto the seat with some difficulty called Blade over and gave him a hell of a pat because he knew his ass had just been saved by his mate. It was some time before he could find the energy to start limping slowly and painfully home leaning heavily on his staff.

No matter how hard Millie nagged him, Jock would not go to the police because he was worried about what might happen to Blade if the story came out. But she had a small victory when he agreed to go to the doctor for a check-up. Here he told a cock-and-bull-story of climbing a fence, slipping and falling down a bank while looking for the dog. The explanation was accepted with a few raised eyebrows but he was sent for an X-ray which revealed severe bruising in the rib, stomach and back areas, but more importantly no breakages. He was informed he'd probably be in pain for a week or so, so he should take it easy, take the prescribed painkillers and rest at home. Millie was disgusted with him for lying to the doctor and even more incensed when he broached a bottle of Bells Scotch Whisky instead of taking the painkillers.

Tracy came over after work and was all for telling Terry, her policeman boyfriend, but saw Jock's point that after all the good and bad publicity for Blade after the attempted burglary, it could well be the straw that broke the camel's back. They also correctly surmised that the four hoods wouldn't want to go to the police either because they were all still supposed to be under some sort of supervision. Later that night, however, Jock rang Tracy and Mac's father and a long conversation ensured.

It was more than a week before he could even consider going for a walk again and even then it was just straight to the park to let Blade off the chain for a long romp. But he soon started to come right again. With the residual fitness of a lifetime kicking in once the pain began to recede. He made sure to keep his eyes peeled while in the park, though. Once bitten, twice shy. But there was no further trouble. Mac and Tracy's Dad came over two weekends later and on the Saturday night the two got into the whisky at Jock's place, talking into the wee small hours.

Jock kept himself pretty quiet for the next few months – so quiet, in fact, that Millie worried about him and wanted him to go back to the doctor for another check-up. But he would not have a bar of that and just told her "hold your whist". She was a bit suspicious at first. The old Jock would have certainly been busting for revenge. But then she thought: "Oh well, maybe he's just getting past it."

The reunion in Palmy in November proved a great success. Being held in the middle of the North Island for a change instead of one of the bigger cities, it was much cheaper to attend and attracted far more people than usual. People just didn't like travelling to the big cities, too much bloody hassle. They caught up with some old mates they hadn't seen for years, found out who was dead, and who was crook, and a lot of metaphorical shrapnel and bullets flew about as the old campaigns were relitigated, some greatly altered and barely recognisable from the original event.

As always, the highly enjoyable weekend fairly flew by and after breakfast and farewells Monday morning Jock and Millie headed home. Millie said she thought it a bit strange they hadn't seen much of Mac and Tracy's Dad on the Saturday night but Jock brushed that off saying that he'd had a bit of the bot and was on antibiotics, which made him very tired so he'd had an early night. The explanation seemed to satisfy Millie.

After arriving home mid-afternoon, they were unloading the car when a police car rocked up the drive and two boys in blue got out. Jock recognised one of them who'd handled Mac and Tracy's break-in.

"Mr Bell," he asked sternly. "Could you tell me where you were on Saturday night please?"

"Aye," replied Jock. "We were in Palmerston North at the Army reunion. Why do you ask?"

"All weekend?"

What do they call answering a question with a question? "Aye, all weekend. Why, what's wrong?"

"There was an assault on Saturday night. One of those four men involved in the attempted burglary of your neighbour's property earlier this year is in a serious condition in hospital and it has been suggested that you may know something about it."

Millie looked as though she was about to say something but Jock held his hand up in a whist motion to her. "Me, the girl and the dog beat the crap out of those thieving scum. Then why would we want to do it again?"

"I don't know," replied the policeman. "We are just following leads at this stage so we would appreciate it if you could give us the details of your time in Palmerston so we can eliminate you from the enquiry."

As Millie headed off inside to get their accommodation receipts and other paperwork, the policeman asked: "Can you think of anyone who might have done it?"

"Aye," said Jock. "Just about anyone whose homes the thieving scum broke into. I'm not fookin' surprised at all. If you wanna kick a dog, you better be ready to get bit. When you find out who did it, shake their hand for me."

This answer just frustrated the copper, who shook his head. Then Millie came out with the details of the weekend and motel receipts, which she handed over. He copied the details into his notebook, handed them back and said: "Thank you for your co-operation. Have a nice day. Oh, and we will check up on your alibi."

"Check-up all you like," replied Jock. "We were there all weekend. There was a ball on Saturday night, went on till after midnight and I was there till the end."

"Thank you for your co-operation sir." The policemen drove away.

Again Millie looked as though she was going to say something but Jock gave her the whist sign again. "Dinna blether," he said gruffly and walked away to show the conversation was over.

The Monday paper was full of it. Around midnight on Saturday, Beau was dropped off at home by one of his mates when a man dressed in black and wearing a black balaclava confronted and smashed him in the kneecap with a baseball bat. This dropped him onto the ground in a screaming pile, and another blow broke his arm. After been given a warning about leaving people and homes alone, he'd been clipped solidly round the head with the bat, certainly not as hard as the other two blows but just enough to stun. Then the man had disappeared as suddenly as he had arrived. The newspaper story said the whole assault had only taken a minute, if that, and the assailant vanished completely, leaving very little in the way of clues with the victim in no condition to be of much use, either. Police were following certain lines of enquiry.

Mac and Tracy were both checked up on as a matter of course, but they had both been at home. With them was Tracy's boyfriend Terry, a policeman. A pretty ironclad alibi, one would have thought.

Beau spent almost three weeks in hospital before being discharged in plaster. The knee injury needed further surgery and caused ongoing discomfort, severely limiting the mobility that is so essential to any would-be burglar.

After two months of fruitless inquiry, it became obvious that the crime would not be solved easily. For many of the burglary victims, it was a case of "who cares, give that man a medal.

Jock and Blade continued on with their walks with no problem whatsoever, and Mac was pleased that he could now travel and not have to worry about Blade. Whenever his job took him to Whanganui or nearby, he always stayed the night with his father. On the next occasion Mac was there, his Dad was out, so he got the key for the garage from where it was hidden and went to get the key for the house from where that was hidden in the garage.

On entering the garage he spied a pair of long black overalls hanging in one of a set of two old lockers his dad had perked from work. In the bottom of the other locker was a pair of army boots. Black too, of course. Suddenly seeing the two items together caused something to ping in Mac's mind. He cast a searching eye around the garage, located several possibilities and began to check them out. It was behind an old fashioned dresser that had been converted into a tool hanging rack his suspicions were confirmed. There was the battered and well-used but still very functional baseball bat from Tracy's school days.

Those pair of hard old bastards, he thought, and they never even breathed a word. With a quiet smile he put the bat back, grabbed the house keys exited and locked the garage, went into the house and waited for his father to get home. The two of them wandered on down to the local pub for a meal and a few beers that night. It was only the next morning, when his Dad came out to see him off, that he wound the window down and said: "By the way, Dad, if I were you I'd lose that baseball bat." You should have seen his father's face drop.

METHOD IN MADNESS

They said old George was bloody mad, and his long white hair and even longer and whiter beard sort of added credibility to the claim. He wore footy shorts, holey T-shirts and Jandals most of the year, even in winter. He seemed impervious to even the deepest cold.

He'd bought the rundown old cottage on the edge of town next to the forest. It had been on the market for years, ever since the old widow who'd owned it had died. Gradually it had become more overgrown, vandalised and used for parties and graffiti practice by the teenagers of the town. The 'for sale' sign had long since disappeared but once George bought it, it was amazing how quickly a new one reappeared with 'sold' and the agent's name on it.

George turned up on a Saturday morning during the school holidays in a truck driven by a young Maori guy, and an accompanying car containing a Maori lady and another man, both in their early 30s, and two pre-teen children. They said these were his kids and his moko. The two guys and the lady got stuck into the house and the property for nearly a month, with an electrician, plumber and other tradesmen parading in and out. Soon the cottage was liveable. It wasn't pretty by any stretch of the imagination, but it was liveable and it was his home. The family got George settled in, then they left.

He kept himself to himself, despite various visitors trying to befriend him or convert him to their particular beliefs. He made it very plain that he preferred his own company. He told them all he was an ex-soldier who thought democracy was a wonderful thing and as long as people didn't break the law or bother anyone else.

You're doing really well so far, he'd tell unwelcome visitors. Most got the message. But soon the rumours started: That he was stark raving mad; that he was an ex-soldier who'd gone to Vietnam as a teenager and what he had seen had turned his mind; that he was an alcoholic (although no one had ever seen him buying alcohol); that he had photos on the wall of the mangled bodies they'd blown up with claymores (though no one had ever seen these photos); that he had nightmares and screamed in his sleep, grinding his teeth; that he'd walk round outside naked and howl at a full moon; that he was a wizard or a warlock and cast magic spells; that he'd go walking in the forest at night to make contact with ghosts or kehua.

Oh yes, there were some fanciful stories about him floating about the town, But they didn't bother old George one little bit. People could believe what they wanted to believe, as long as they left him alone. Every few weeks, his daughter would come and do his shopping, leaving his moko with him to look after while she was in town. People said that they wouldn't let him look after their grandchildren. He was mad, they said.

The only other person George ever really saw was Toi, another Vietnam vet who lived locally. The two had served up top together, seen a bit of shit and made a good pair, everyone said, because Toi could be a bit mad himself at times. Or so they said. The two got together on Anzac Day, drank the RSA out of rum and got legless. Someone told them they were just a pair of alcoholics. George replied that while he wasn't an alcoholic, he had gone on the whiskey diet once. He said he hadn't lost much weight but his mind had gone AWOL for a week or so. Toi cracked up. Eventually they had to be helped into the car taken home by Toi's daughter, who happened to be visiting. How she got them out of the RSA and into the car remained a mystery. I wouldn't want to have to go home with those two, people said. They're both mad. But old George and Toi, they didn't worry none about that shit. Sticks and stones; sticks and stones.

A drug dealer moved into the town and before long there were all sorts of beaten up old cars with no warrants or regos beating a path to the somewhat isolated house the dealer rented. Any time of day or night, you could see people and cars buzzing up and down that driveway like bees at a hive. Then there was noise from the wild parties just about every weekend as well. Kids in school uniform, riding bikes or pushing scooters were seen going in and out, and the neighbourhood suddenly seemed to be attracting all sorts of rough and odd-looking drongos. Some were knocking on the wrong doors, disturbing the elderly and asking for drugs. A spate of burglaries occurred and many younger people in the town were implicated. Stealing to get money to buy drugs.

Tut, tut, they said, what are the police doing about it? Nothing because they're underage and the law can't touch them, the police said. But then the law must be bullshit, they said.

Old George's house didn't get burgled, they left him well alone. Don't go near him, he's stark raving mad. You wouldn't know what goes on in there, they said.

A girl was raped at one of the parties and it was someone who lived in the drug house that did it, they all said. Police investigated but couldn't find enough evidence to prosecute. She'd asked for it by going there in the first place, people said. A month or so later, the girl committed suicide. She was Toi's moko and he was greatly upset. After the tangi, Toi came round to George's place, where he finally broke down and cried.

George was upset for his old mate so he wrote a letter to another of his old army mates.

About a week later, a car came to his house late at night and someone handed him a package. The next day, George told Toi to go and stay with his daughter for a while. A few days later, he ran into the drug dealer in town and couldn't resist having words with him about the girl. "Fuck off, you mad old bugger," the drug dealer said. "Ha ha ha, you can fuckin' suck my cock. She did." And he strode off dismissing George as a nothing. Shaking his head sadly, George finally made his mind up.

Dressed in black and utilizing the shadows to good effect, he slipped up the driveway at 0233 hrs the following morning. He'd OPed the place since nightfall and thought his man should now be in there alone. In gloved hands he carried a crowbar and a rock, with a special and final surprise stuck in his belt. He fired the rock through the kitchen window and quickly took position to the side of the back door, crowbar raised. When the dealer came rushing out to investigate, he was smashed right where the neck and shoulder join. He didn't even see it coming. It dropped him screaming to the ground, and when he saw George standing over him, he screamed out.

"You fuckin' old prick, I'll... " The screaming died abruptly when he saw what George's now held in his hand. "What? What the fuck? "Real fear erupted on to his face

"Hey, boy," said George. "You know how you said she sucked your cock? Well now you can suck my Glock."

Quickly rolling him over so the back of his head was on the ground, George pushed the pistol right into the disbelieving mouth and fired the one shot. Rolling the body out of the way, he used the crowbar to quickly dig the spent round out. After a quick look around to make sure to coast was clear and that he had left nothing behind, he padded softly into the shadow of the night.

They didn't discover the body till after daylight and the news quickly spread through the town. Drug dealers were well known to be armed, paranoid and violent when protecting their supplies and patch, so a rival drug dealer had done it, they said. It was gang-related, they said. A dissatisfied user had done it, they said.

The police inquiries followed all the normal possibilities but got nowhere. Toi was spoken to when the circumstances of his moko's death came to light, but of course he had been out of town. There was a whole big forest to hide a pistol, crowbar and spent round in and, anyway, no one ever thought mad old George could do a thing like that. The police eventually got to him in the course of their inquiries, but they told themselves: "Nah, he could never have done it. Too bloody old and too bloody mad to be doing that sort of shit." They never ever found the weapon or the killer. And Toi never said anything, either. He just came round and hongied his mate. That about said it all, I reckon.

And George, bloody mad old George? Well, he wasn't too mad to get away with murder was he? Actually, he probably thought he was doing the country a favour and just did what he was trained to do. If you could ever get him to talk about it, he'd probably say it wasn't a murder, it was merely an expediency. Or "just getting rid of a wasta a fuckin' rations", as a grunt would have put it. And the cops seem to be too busy raising money off speeding motorists to be worried about the drug dealers trying to hook our kids these days, don't they? So maybe old George wasn't that mad, after all. But one thing is for sure: He wasn't really much of a poet, was he?

MAKING AN HONEST LIVING

WHAT'S GOOD FOR THE GOOSE

It just didn't seem right somehow, no matter which way he looked at it. Joe Travers, rookie real estate salesman, shook his head in frustration. He was sorely puzzled. He had a copy of the company rules on commission splits in front of him. Everything pointed to him having been entitled to at least half a share of the sales commission on this particular deal, not just the quarter he had received. The difference was a matter of $700 – "only" $700, as the firm's top salesperson, Karen, had so dismissively pointed out after he queried what he'd been awarded for selling her sole agency listing. But it was all right for her to consider the shortfall peanuts. She was on megabucks compared to him, aided by a higher percentage split with the company because of the volume of real estate she turned over.

Joe had been in the game for only four months and had really been battling to get any sort of a deal away for more than two months now. It had been a hard grind since the two easy sales he'd started off with. They'd been a shoo-in because it was his sister and brother-in-law selling then buying through him. Their home had been his very first sole agency and another of the company's agents had an offer on the table within a week. Then his sister and her husband had themselves found the place they wanted to buy and had just gone through him to do the deal. Real easy, this real estate game, he'd thought back then. He'd been struggling ever since.

Again, he went over the events leading up to his present

predicament. He'd met the buyers, a young couple, at one of his open homes and there'd been an instant rapport. They wanted to work through Joe because, they said, he wasn't the least bit pushy. They told him a lot of other agents had pestered the hell out of them. They had already decided their preferred and absolute top price range, approaching it with refreshing realism. They realised they would only be able to afford a doer-upper so they wanted to keep money in reserve for the alterations and decorating they expected they'd have to do. They were both working six days a week, building up their funds while they were still childless. They didn't have much spare time and they asked Joe to do the homework for them.

At about the same time, Karen had signed up a place on sole agency which really looked like it might fit the bill. It wasn't an expensive property by any stretch of the imagination, a classic doer upper in need of a fair bit of TLC. An ideal first home for a young couple with a not very large deposit, limited in what they could borrow and expecting to start a family at any tick of the clock.

They were only available to view on a Sunday, which was generally when Joe was busy with his own open homes. So he'd booked them in to view Karen's property as his buyers, a perfectly normal and acceptable practice in the real estate world. They'd been accepted as his buyers, which meant they could view the home without him being present. So they went and had look and could immediately see the potential. They decided to put in an offer on the spot. And that was where all the trouble had started.

Because she had a lot of sole agencies and probably because this was a cheaper property as well, Karen had used another person, a lesser light called Sheila, to run this open home. This was another normal practice. Sheila would hope to find a buyer herself and pick up a share of the commission. But instead of ringing to tell Joe that his buyers wanted to put in the offer and then waiting for him to arrive, Sheila immediately drew up a contract and got the young couple to sign it. Then, with Karen's permission but without telling Joe, she presented it to the owners.

By the time Joe came on to the scene, the owners had already countersigned the contract at a slightly higher price and all that remained for him to do was to go back to his young couple and get them to agree. This they duly did, because when they made their original offer, they had allowed for some price negotiation.

Yes, deal done and a good buy for his young couple, Joe thought at the time. He worked out his share of the commission would be roughly $1400. But as it was Karen's sole agency, it was up to her to complete the paperwork for the splitting of the commission – and when Joe's cheque arrived, it was for only half the expected amount.

In normal circumstances, Sheila would be entitled to half the commission because she had sold the property at an open home she ran on behalf of the sole agent. But in this case, the buyers were Joe's and he had properly booked them in for the open home, as the rules required. So he actually should have received a full half share. Sheila had overplayed her hand in starting the deal without waiting for Joe.

Whatever Karen decided to award Sheila, it should have come out of her share of the commission, not Joe's. When he queried the anomaly with Karen, she cattily said he'd done very little to assist the sale and should count himself lucky to be even getting a share at all. Not surprisingly, Sheila wholeheartedly agreed. Karen also suggested that that if Joe complained to the boss, he might lose his share altogether.

Joe wasn't real happy with the situation and after a couple of days chewing it over finally approached the boss. He had already been told by the two women that Joe might raise the subject and wasn't keen to become involved, especially as he was engrossed in a big commercial deal.

It was clear that Karen and Sheila had ever so slightly bent the facts in their story to the boss. Joe tried to push his case that he had followed company protocols and Sheila should not have started the deal without him. But the boss was not interested in pursuing the matter further. He was loath to rule against Karen, who had threatened to leave on several occasions. She would be made extremely welcome at any other company in town. Reluctantly, Joe decided to chalk it up to experience – a rather expensive lesson to the tune of some $700. But like an elephant, he wouldn't forget it.

Two and a Half Years Later

"Thanks Bryce," said Joe. "I really appreciate you putting your trust in me."

"That's all right, mate," came the reply. "You've earned it with all the work you've done at the rugby club and the support your company has given us."

"Our pleasure," said Joe. "I'll contact you later re the open homes once it's all sorted out and I'll be back later to put the sign up."

"Whatever," said Bryce. "But you better talk to the missus about the open homes first before you plan one. Knowing her, she'll want the bloody place spotless."

"Okay," said Joe. "Hopefully she'll be home when I come back to put the sign up and take the photos. Thanks again, mate."

"Hey, I wouldn't give it to anyone else. You're the man. I gotta go, see you later."

Joe was rapt. Another sole agency. Bryce was the president of the rugby club he belonged to and where he had coached kids' teams for past six years or so.

Eighteen months previously, he and the boss came up with a deal that if any member of the club bought or sold their property through Joe on sole agency, the company would donate $500 to the club. Half of this amount would come from Joe's share of the commission and half from the company's share. So he wasn't losing much anyway.

The scheme had worked well so far. If he did manage to sell Bryce's home it would be the fifth $500 payout, an enormous help in a small, always cash-strapped club. Then if Bryce bought again through him, which was quite on the cards as well, there'd be another $500 for the club. The way Joe saw it, it didn't really cost him anything because it only had to be paid if he earned something. As far as he was concerned it was a win/win for both him and the club.

Joe had actually been doing really well in the real estate game for 18 months now. After an initial struggle and a lot of doubts, things had finally fallen into place. He'd developed his own operating style, taking a laid-back approach with both sellers and buyers that had worked really well. It also helped that he was not afraid to discount a bit of commission to make a deal happen.

He was getting a lot of referrals from satisfied clients and was also starting to generate a fair amount of repeat business. One of his biggest successes had been his listing strategy. Whenever vendors told him that they needed yay amount for their home or they wouldn't sell, he'd simply recite his three rules of real estate:

1.   A property's worth what someone is willing to pay for it.
2.   A prospective purchaser is entitled to make an offer.
3.   The owner doesn't have to accept the offer.

Joe repeated these rules again and again to his vendors and buyers. If a vendor ever went crook at him for bringing them a lower-than-expected offer, he'd simply ask: "What are the three rules of real estate that I've been quoting to you from day one?" This generally had the desired effect.

With more sales successes, Joe was now company's fifth-highest commission earner and not too far behind the front-runners, pretty good in a 15-strong sales team. He was also the top sole agency lister – but generally of less expensive properties, mostly the homes of the working-class people that he knew through rugby. But these were the properties that turned over more frequently. And as his dear old mum always used to say, a bob in the hand is worth two in the bush.

Karen was still the top salesperson but not by such a wide margin now. A couple of others were making a strong rush at what had been an almost unassailable position. She was still the same, though, a real prima donna, stressed out much of the time, always shaking nervously and smoking like a train when a deal was being negotiated. Still loved getting it all her own way, too, and so quick to run to the boss if she perceived someone else gaining what she considered an unfair advantage over her.

Joe had had a good laugh one time when he received a sole agency from an RSA mate, ex-military like him. The property was actually rented out to friends of Karen's. When she found out it was coming on to the market with him as the sole agent, she had immediately complained to the boss that it should have been hers because she knew the tenants. Joe had just laughed and asked her if the tenants were going to sign any offer received, which didn't go down that well at all and was the subject of yet another complaint. He generally steered as well clear of her as he could, finding her far too intense, selfish and greedy for his liking. Most of the other staff felt the same.

Joe worked Bryce's property for just over a month before finally securing an offer. It wasn't a bad one either, only $6000 below the asking price, subject only to finance, the permits being up to scratch and the usual legalities. He was rapt as he got the contract drawn up on the Monday morning. The buyers were his too, so if he could put the deal together he would get all the commission.

Once he had the offer signed by the buyers, he rang Bryce at work and made an appointment to see him and his wife as soon as they were both available. That turned out to be in the evening when they both got home from work, so Joe carried on with his Monday routine – preparing feedback to vendors from the previous weekend's open homes and writing ads for the following weekend. Then came another offer for Bryce's property – unfortunately from buyers who were Karen's. The boss's ears pricked up when he was told there were two offers on the table for the same property. With total fairness in mind for both sets of buyers, he instructed Joe and Karen to go back to their respective clients, tell them there were now two offers on the same property, and say they should put their best offer on the table.

Joe's buyers came up with another $2000, which he thought would be acceptable to Bryce and his wife. As the sole agent for the property, it was his job to present any offers and he was staggered to find that Karen's buyers were offering exactly the same amount as his and subject to the same conditions, finance and permits.

Meanwhile, Karen had complained to the boss about Joe presenting her offer as well as his own, saying she'd rather present hers in person. The boss ruled that although it was Joe's sole agency and therefore his prerogative to present any offers, on this occasion Joe had a vested interest and perhaps it would be fairer and better if a third party presented both offers.

Joe was reluctant. Bryce was his friend and had really expected to be dealing only with Joe. The boss said okay but what if he rang Bryce and explained the situation and he was agreeable. Joe reluctantly agreed and in the event Bryce did understand and was happy for a third party to present the offers, as long as Joe and the rugby club still got paid.

"No worries about that," said the boss as he hung up. But who would do the honours? The boss obviously thought of himself as the natural choice. Joe had other ideas, though. He nominated Bob, one of their rural salesman, an ex-navy and rugby man. Joe thought he and Bryce would get along famously, and so Bob was appointed.

The next step was for Karen and Joe to go one at a time into Bob's office to explain their offer. Karen went first, and Joe thought hard until she finally emerged with a self-satisfied smirk on her face. Then Joe went in and explained his offer. He said Bob could tell Bryce that if his offer was accepted, he would knock a further $500 off the commission. In his mind, this was far better than losing the $2000-plus he would if he had to share with Karen. And anyway, commission reductions were generally shared dollar-for-dollar with the company, so he'd actually lose only $250 anyway. Bob cracked a mile wide smile at this. He'd had a few run-ins with Karen himself and didn't much like her. "You cunning bastard," was all he said, and didn't mention a word of this to anyone. As Joe had known he wouldn't. Of course, who in their right mind wouldn't want to save another $500? Bryce and his wife quickly accepted Joe's offer and were more than happy to do so.

Joe was contacted later on that night by both Bob and Bryce informing him of the decision. Bryce was excited about the deal and the saving he'd made on the commission. Bob warned him, however, that you-know-who had given him a right earful when she found her offer had missed out.

When Karen found out from her office spy that it was the commission reduction that had made the difference, she exploded and immediately went to the boss to complain. Again.

Joe arrived at work the next morning to find a rather irate female raving on about integrity, cheats, level playing fields, under-handed tricks, money hunger and even going so far as calling into question the legitimacy of his heritage. Joe didn't say much. As far as he was concerned, there was still a way to go before the deal became unconditional. So he just smiled sweetly at her, which seemed to make her worse, almost apoplectic in fact.

When the boss arrived, he took Karen outside to cool off. Having done that, with some difficulty, he called Joe into his office. He said he'd had her on the phone for almost two hours the previous evening ranting and raving and threatening to leave if he didn't do something about the situation. He couldn't do much about the deal, as it was already signed up. But if she did leave the company, it would be entirely Joe's fault.

He said Joe had not done anything illegal and in fact it was his normal practice to discount commission. But it was definitely a curve ball, almost but not quite underhanded. The boss asked Joe why he'd done it, given his history of strict fairness in every action. Joe reminded the boss of how Karen duped him out of $700 when he first started. This was his way of paying her back. The boss couldn't even remember the occasion, having been far too preoccupied to take much notice at the time. Nevertheless, he congratulated Joe and said he hoped the sale went through. But if it did, he added sternly, the $500 discount should come solely from his share of the sale and not the company's. Joe agreed to this with a big smile on his face. The sale eventually went unconditional and settled just over a month later.

When Joe worked out the commission sheet, he somehow cleanly forgot the boss's instruction to take the discount off his share only and halved it with the company as normal. Whether the boss picked this omission up when he checked the paperwork, Joe never bothered to ask. But when the cheque did finally arrive, it was only $250 off what he would normally have got. So things were looking pretty good. Bryce did buy through him again, the rugby club did well again, and so did Joe.

And just to let you know, Joe did allow himself the luxury of a small gloat. On the day he got the cheque, he went to Karen's desk, flapped it about and said: "Hey, remember that time you did me out of $700? Well, I just about tripled that on you."

He moved away before the explosion and threw back over his shoulder: "You should always remember, what's good for the goose."

He didn't bother to finish another of his mother's old adages. He just kept walking, humming happily as he made his way down to the bank. Two weeks later, Karen left. She was sorely missed by no one.

DON'T JUDGE A BOOK BY ITS COVER

Joe was out on the deck nursing a beer and mulling over a property he'd just listed. It had been on the market with various other agents for more than 18 months with never even a hint of an offer. Suddenly his phone rang. It was Lance, an acquaintance from the RSA and an ex-military man like Joe. It seemed his parents had had their property on the market with another firm and an offer had come in for it, but there was some sort of hiccup and his parents wanted advice.

Joe sighed. It wasn't really his place to go meddling in another company's affairs and there'd be absolutely nothing in it for him. But old Lance wasn't a bad lad so as a favour, he reluctantly agreed to go and see them the next morning. The property was an absolute beauty, a real pleasure to behold. It was an immaculately presented 1960s three-bedroom weatherboard home with an attached self-contained granny flat that had been added on later. The 800-plus square metre section was ideally situated for the early morning sun and had a lovely rural outlook. Completing the picture was a huge double garage with workshop and fully lined sleep-out, plus generous basement storage space under the granny flat. Setting off the idyllic scene were exceptional vegetable and flower gardens flourishing in the rich black volcanic soil, with just about every kind of fruit tree or vine you could imagine, including a thriving banana tree in the hothouse.

Joe was suitably impressed as he was shown around by Lance's parents, who were salt-of-the earth country people. Sprightly and plainly dressed, Harry and Mildred were in their 80s and had bought the property 10 years earlier on retirement from the farm.

Harry was a World War II veteran and had won the farm block in a ballot, but it had taken all his working life to turn the mainly bush acreage into a viable farming proposition. When Lance had shown no interest in taking over, they'd sold the farm on a somewhat depressed market and moved into town. They'd enjoyed their time there, they said, and would be sad to leave. But it had become too much for them to manage as they'd got older and they now had to downsize.

After the grand tour, they moved on to the deck and while Harry and Joe engaged in small talk, Mildred busied herself producing a real country-style morning tea – home-made scones with jam and cream and aromatic tea poured from a huge antique porcelain teapot.

As Mildred finally sat down, Joe opened the conversation. "Before we start," he said, "I'd better tell you that theoretically, I shouldn't be here at all, as it is another company's sole agency. But, as Lance's friend, I may be able to make some suggestions.

"There are three rules I always abide by when dealing with real estate. I think if you listen to them, you might understand better where I'm coming from. Do you mind if I run through them for you?"

Both nodded and he continued.

"Rule number one: a property is worth what someone will pay for it. Rule number two: buyers are entitled to make an offer. Rule number three: the owner does not have to accept the offer. I recite these time and again, to both vendors and buyers, so when things do happen, they are in no doubt of where they stand. Do you understand where I'm coming from?"

Both nodded. In his unhurried speaking style, Harry said: "That's the cause of all the trouble we're having, Joe. The firm we're dealing with doesn't seem to have heard of that third rule. Here, take a look at this."

He passed Joe a document that proved to be a recent private valuation from a reputable local firm, suggesting the property's value on the present market should be somewhere around the $220,000 mark.

"Can't argue with that, from what I've seen," said Joe.

"Take a look at this, then," said Harry and passed over a contract.

It was an offer for \$175,000 for the property, subject only to finance, which was apparently pre-approved anyway, according to the agents, and a Land Information Report which was a standard safeguard generally recommended by most lawyers.

"They told us it was a virtual cash offer and we shouldn't countersign it or we might lose the buyers," Harry said.

Mildred butted in: "It's not even enough to allow us to get the place we've got the conditional offer on, and who's going to give us a mortgage at our age? We might as well stay on here."

Joe was nonplussed. "Hang on, hang on," he said. "You mean they wouldn't let you countersign the contract at a higher amount?"

"More or less," said Harry. "In fact, they were downright pushy. Wanted us to sign it on the spot. Got a bit snarky when we wouldn't, especially the woman. She's a bit of a Tartar."

"They were so nice when we listed with them and signed up on the other place," said Mildred. "But they certainly changed when we wouldn't sign the offer. The buyers seemed to be friends of theirs, from what they were saying."

Joe shook his head. He knew the couple in question, a husband-and-wife team renowned as brutal price-crunchers when they got an offer. They were bullish negotiators and especially harsh on vendors. The truth of the matter was that it was actually the vendors who paid the commission, and it was for them they should try to get the best price possible.

The wife was indeed a real Tartar, especially when she couldn't get her own way. One of his colleagues had once rather uncharitably described her as old mutton in lamb's clothing. He'd have to be extremely careful what he suggested here, though, because here he was involved another company's sole agency, offering advice on their offer. The much-talked-about but, in Joe's opinion, rather-too-often-not-adhered-to Real Estate Code of Ethics must also be followed. He chose his next words carefully.

"In my opinion" he said, "you should counter-sign this offer at an amount that is acceptable to you. If the buyers won't come up to what you will accept, ask the agents to tell them to find another house. You might also remind them who is paying their commission while you're at it, too."

"Do you think it will be all right?" Mildred asked. "They

definitely changed once they brought the offer. I didn't much like their attitude to much at all."

"Well if they do give you any trouble, you're quite entitled to withdraw your property off the market, you know, but you can't list it with any other company until their sole agency period is up, that's all".

"Good, I'm glad you told me that," said a happier looking Harry. "I'll ring them this afternoon, and if the buyers won't come up or they give us any more stick, we'll withdraw the property. There's still two months to run on their listing but I've just about had a gutsful of them anyway."

He glanced at his wife, who nodded, somehow knowing what he was going to say. "You don't want to sell it for us, do you Joe?" he asked. "I'd rather have someone I can talk to, to handle it."

"I'd love to," said Joe. "But I can't do anything until their sole agency expires. And anyway, you should really see if the buyers will come up. Who knows? They might just surprise you. Try that first and see what happens."

"All right," said Harry. "But if they give us any problem at all, I'm going to withdraw it from the market and give it to you when the times up. Okay?"

"I'd be happy to have it. But, look, give it a go. You never know. And good luck anyway," said Joe.

That seemed to about complete the business end of matters, so they turned to the delicious morning tea spread in front of them. Joe left nearly an hour later, uncomfortably full of rich country-style food and totally impressed with both Harry and Mildred. They might speak slowly and seem like simple country folk, but he'd found them very intelligent and knowledgeable – people not to be taken lightly. It reminded him very much of one of his mother's old sayings: Still water runs deep.

That night after work, Joe turned off his mobile phone and went to the golf club for a quiz night, totally forgetting about the day's events. He didn't know that Harry had rung the agents and informed them that he and Mildred had counter-signed the contract at $220,000 and that they could come and pick it up. This information didn't seem to impress the female agent one little bit. Harsh words were spoken. Then Harry, speaking in the simple, direct and truthful way often found among country people, unwittingly put Joe into a fair spot of bother.

"We've spoken to Joe Travers from Smithson's Real Estate, and he tells us that we are quite entitled to counter-sign at whatever amount we wish. He also said that you should be trying to get us the best price possible, because we are paying your commission, and that if your buyers won't come up to our price, then to tell them to find another house."

Loud and angry words erupted from the other end of the phone. Harry responded: "Well, if that's your attitude, I'll thank you to come and get your signs. Joe told us we could withdraw our property from you whenever we wished. I've taken them down already, anyway, and if they're not gone by tomorrow morning I'll put them on the bonfire. Good day to you" He hung up on the thoroughly exasperated agent.

Joe rose early next morning as usual and headed off to the office. He always liked to be first there because he reckoned he thought best when it was quiet, especially when there were ads to write. He got quite a surprise on arrival, though, because waiting impatiently for him was none other than the male half of the pair trying to sell Harry and Mildred's place. The flustered receptionist had had the misfortune to find him on the doorstep when she'd arrived to open up.

"What right have you," he thundered before Joe could even say a word, "to interfere in one of our sole agencies? That old couple has lost the deal and withdrawn their property now. I'll report you to the institute. What you've done is unethical! You'll lose your real estate ticket! I ought to punch you in the nose!"

He raved on all the time closing on the bewildered Joe, who in recognising a threat, turned sideways, looking harshly at the other agent and cocking his fist. This overtly aggressive action stopped the other agent in his tracks, but he still kept raving on.

Joe slowly began to realise what had happened. Old Harry must have been a bit too straight with them, he thought. He began to speak. "Listen, mate!" he said. "If you've lost the deal and a sole agency, it's because you didn't do the job right and not because of anything I've done. Those people asked me for advice, and I gave it. You should be a bit more careful about how you treat your clients. I think you've forgotten who pays the commission. And as for telling them they couldn't counter-sign the offer, that really sucks, especially if the buyers are friends of yours".

"That old couple wouldn't know zip. They're just a pair of old hayseeds," burst in the other agent. "And you've been unethical in talking to them when it's none of your business."

"I reckon it's you who's been unethical," Joe retorted. "You tried to rip them off and now you come in here threatening me. I think you should leave now before you get yourself into trouble." With that, he started crowding his opposite to the door.

"I want to talk to Barry! I want to lay a complaint!" the other blustered.

"He'll be in this afternoon. Ring him then. You're not welcome here" said Joe, giving the agent just a gentle nudge down the stairs."

"You'll be hearing from us and the institute," the other man blustered from the safety of the bottom of the stairs.

"Good, I'll look forward to it, then," said Joe. Then almost entirely involuntarily, out it came: "And tell your bloody wife that she's nothing but a pair of painted pantyhose full of shit anyway."

He closed the door firmly to be met by an amused but concerned receptionist. "I can't believe you just did and said that, Joe. You know there's going to be trouble now, don't you?"

"Yeah, I know," said Joe, already regretting his outburst. "They're just a bunch of arseholes, anyway." He disappeared almost nonchalantly into his cubicle, but he was worried that he had rather overstepped the mark. He knew he'd be hearing more about it.

"What am I going to do with you, Joe?" Barry asked, shaking his head. "You threw him out the door, you insulted his wife, you lost them a deal and a sole agency. There will be trouble, you know. You and I will probably have to front up to the institute."

"I'm sorry for the trouble here, boss," said Joe. "But as far as I'm concerned, they didn't do the right thing by the old couple and deserved to lose their agency. I'll tell that to the Institute, too. You know you're always telling us to look after the vendors and that's all I did. I told them your rules and what they could and couldn't do."

"Yes, but it wasn't our sole agency," said Barry. "You didn't have to become involved."

"Boss, they asked me for advice and I gave it as honestly as I could, and apart from what happened here, anything else they brought on themselves. How good would it look if it became known that real estate agents ripped off an old couple? And she's even got the cheek to give a talk about the code of ethics at an REINZ meeting. I'll stand by what I did, even if I do get booted out."

Barry shook his head. "I don't want to lose you, Joe. You're the best lister in the company. But it might well come to that, unfortunately. They've got clout. What about apologising?"

"No way, boss" said Joe. "I'll hang before I do that."

The boss picked up his phone still shaking his head. "You may well have to yet. I'll see what I can do, but I'm not real hopeful." He motioned for Joe to leave.

"They've put in a complaint all right, Joe" said Barry. "Wanted you suspended till the hearing, too, but I managed to put the kibosh on that. We have to front up at the next meeting in three weeks' time. I'm not too hopeful, though. They've just about charged you with every breach of the code of ethics in the book. Do you think the old couple will help out?"

"I don't really want to bother them, boss," said Joe. "They've got enough hassles at this stage, especially at their age. No, I think I'd rather leave them out of it for now. Look, I'm sure everything is going to work out all right. I'll catch you later."

All the same, he wasn't that confident and events over the following week seemed to bear this pessimism out.

It was as though he had become a leper overnight. News of the charges got around real estate circles as if by magic. The husband-and-wife team did a good job of character assassination, too, and the events became remarkably embellished in the telling and retelling. Previously friendly colleagues from other companies studiously avoided him. Coincidentally or not, inquiries about his listings dried up, new properties always seemed to go to the other companies' agents and he began to wonder whether they were using the fact that he was facing charges against him. Several of the vendors of his sole agencies also withdrew their properties from the market with no explanation and worst of all, the phone just ceased to ring. It was a really worrying time for him and he even began to read the situations vacant ads in the local paper. Even Joe himself believed he would probably get his real estate ticket revoked.

"I don't know how you did it, Joe," said Barry a fortnight later. "But the complaint has been withdrawn. Apparently a letter was received from the old couple, which I was not allowed to sight, and that brought about the turnaround. Not only that, but you are allowed to list the property as a sole agency immediately. You've got the luck of the Irish, Joe. I thought you were gone for all money."

"So did I boss," said Joe, feeling a lot more relieved than he let on. "I'll go and thank them right now." He disappeared, leaving the boss still scratching his head. "Get them some flowers on the company account," Barry yelled as an afterthought. But Joe had bolted.

The letters were extremely well done. There was one from both Harry and Mildred, each casting serious doubts on the honesty and integrity of the husband-and-wife team. Each also asked what sort of people would attempt to put one over an old couple in an endeavour to get sales, and queried whether they were fit people to be in such a business. It was also suggested that a letter to the local paper would be on the agenda if Joe were further victimised for merely giving the advice that they'd asked for in the first place, anyway.

The real coup in Joe's mind, and probably the final convincer in the institute's decision, was in the heading of each letter. It seemed there was a lot more to Harry and Mildred than met the eye, just as Joe had first suspected. Harry's letter was headed 'Major Harold Bettison, MM. (retd)' and Mildred's was headed 'Mrs Mildred Bettison, MBE'.

It was a real surprise to Joe and would have been to the institute as well. As his old Irish mum had always used to say, you should never judge a book by its cover.

Joe listed the property and, being ex-army himself, enjoyed some brilliant military conversations with Harry over the selling period. He found out from Lance that his father had won the MM for conspicuous gallantry in the desert during World War II and his mum was honoured her tireless work on the home front during the same period. The property eventually sold for $217,000 – not quite the $220,000 they wanted but near enough, especially when Joe dropped $1000 off the commission.

They missed out on the property they had the conditional offer on but Joe got to work and found them an almost completed townhouse. The developer needed a quick sale to allow him to move on to the next one of three he was building on the same site, and didn't want to borrow any more money. Harry and Mildred got their new place for $180,000, which gave them a pleasing amount left in their kick, and they were already looking forward to planning their new garden, albeit on a much smaller scale. Perhaps that was the secret of longevity, Joe thought, always having something to look forward to. He'd ponder on that one.

When he helped Lance move his parents into their new home, the builder was so impressed he gave Joe the sole agency on the second one, on which he'd already started work. Joe was rapt. He told Barry he was thinking of sending a thank-you card to the other agents. "Don't you bloody dare!" the boss growled.

What a pity though, Joe thought, that some agents couldn't abide by their own code of ethics. It only took one to give them all a bad name, but he knew that there was more than one out there. Oh well, he thought, what goes round comes round, or as the Bible said, as you sow, so shall you reap.

The other agents certainly reaped beggar all out of that deal that was for sure, whereas he had come up with a gold ring on his nose for once. And as for Harry and Mildred, well you surely shouldn't judge a book by its cover, that's for sure.

FAMILY WHEN IT SUITS

"While you're doing that, you might as well take a run out to Blakesbrough and deliver this to Diane's brother. He's got that big trucking business out there." Mandy handed Geoff a parcel wrapped in Christmas paper. It looked and felt suspiciously like a box of chocolates, and he shook it to confirm that's what it was.

"Yeah, we can do that," he replied. "They'll all enjoy a bit of a run in the country for a change, I reckon. Except Fred, of course. He'll just go to sleep as usual. Wish I had his system. What's the go with the choccies, then?"

"Oh, that's just my little annual Christmas stir," replied Mandy. "Diane's brother hasn't been to see her for about four years. Actually, he didn't really come that much even when their parents were still alive. When we took her to their Mum's funeral, he didn't even acknowledge her, and he's never visited once since."

"That's a bit sad," said Geoff. "So you're sort of like saying, 'hey, she's still here, you bastard'."

Mandy laughed. "Well, yes I suppose so, but I would have put it a bit more delicately than that." They both laughed.

"Oh, by the way," she continued, "at the house meeting yesterday – you know, the one you couldn't attend."

This last bit was emphasized because Geoff was not noted for his regular attendance at the bi-weekly meetings.

"Yes," Geoff said, with a big smile at the not-so-subtle dig.

"Well, we've all decided to put in for the big Lotto jackpot on Saturday. Do you want to be in?"

"We've as much chance of winning as a person walking out in the open air has of being struck on the head with porcine excrement," scoffed Geoff. "But yes, I'll be in."

"Why Geoffrey!" said Mandy. "That's very coarse and cynical. What would your mother say?"

They both cracked up because when he had started work there and Mandy had been calling him Geoffrey, he'd told her that only his mother called him that and then only when he was in the shit.

"Hey," said Geoff when they'd stopped laughing. "Why don't we put the clients in too? You never know, they might even bring us some luck. Shit, we've never had any yet."

"I don't see why not, but I'll have to see Mary about it first, though. She's the financial lady," said Mandy. "I know William likes to have a bit of a flutter. I took him to the races once and he had a ball, made about 20 bucks putting a dollar each way on number four in every race. I don't think she'll quibble if they all put in $2 each, but I'll check first though, okay?"

"Done," said Geoff and delved into his pocket. "Have we got a name for our syndicate?"

"I was going to call it the Cilly Syndicate."

"What about the silly Cilly Syndicate?"

"That's not a silly idea," replied Mandy.

They both laughed again.

Geoff and Mandy worked for CIL Services Ltd, short for Community Integrated Living. It provided people with intellectual disabilities enough support to enable them to live within the community rather than being institutionalized as they had been in the past.

There were five clients living in the house – Fred, Murray, William and Jack, with just the one female, Diane. It was actually a very good balance of people. A lot of forethought and planning went into managing the house, and generally they all got on well together, apart from the odd spat, which is pretty normal in life. Geoff had only been working in the house for some 11 months, but Mandy had had nearly 10 years' experience, most of that time at this house where there'd been only one change of client. She really knew them all rather well.

Apart from Fred, aged around 40 and with Down Syndrome, the rest were in their mid-50s and upwards, with Jack the oldest at 64, but still very spry and wiry even though he ate like a horse. They all ate very well, actually. In fact, meal time was probably the highlight of their day. The only one who seemed to put on weight was Fred, with possibly the Down Syndrome element having something to do with that.

Geoff smiled when he remembered the time when one of the local churches invited their clients to a service and a shared lunch afterwards. When a lady turned up in a van to pick them up, he'd told her to give them only a reasonable amount of food and no more, or they'd eat till they became ill. She'd replied: "Oh, they wouldn't, would they?" He'd assured her that they would and when she dropped them off later that afternoon, she was shaking her head in disbelief. "You were right," she'd said. "I've never seen anyone eat like that before."

"They certainly love their food," he replied. "It's the main pleasure in their lives."

Apart from when they were asleep, the only time the house was relatively quiet was at meal time, when everyone was getting on with the serious business of eating.

Geoff glanced into the rear-vision mirror. Yep, as he had suspected, Fred was nodding off already. He had this amazing and enviable ability to drop off to sleep anywhere and anytime. He checked further down the back of the vehicle to make sure Murray, the rebel of the group, still had his seatbelt done up. Mostly their clients were pretty easy to look after but if there was any trouble, you could be sure Murray would be involved somewhere. He could be as stubborn as Paddy's pigs but over the months, the two had built up a bit of rapport with boundaries set and respected by both. So they didn't have too many disagreements these days.

In his earlier days, Geoff had been in the army and he reckoned that the clients were easier to look after than some of the soldiers he had trained. William was a bit of a card, too. The only one who could speak readily, he always had a comment to make or a question to ask and Geoff quite often gave stupid answers. But the caregiver had been caught out beautifully recently. They had all been picked up for Sunday morning service as usual, which was great for the staff on duty because it gave them a free run on the housework.

Geoff had been preparing lunch when they came back and William had said: "Hey Geoff, we've been to church. Been to church. We're back now."

Being a bit of a smartie, Geoff had answered: "Hey man, did you see God?"

William had answered: "Yeah, we saw God."

So Geoff had asked: "What did He say?" The reply flabbergasted him: "He said He likes you." That completely stuffed him up.

He smiled at that recollection, then his mind turned on the errand they were on and he shook his head sadly. In general, most families didn't seem to care too much about their more unfortunate brothers or sisters, especially after the parents died. They were visited very seldom if at all, with the odd birthday or Christmas card arriving but generally no sort of contact at all. That was apart from Fred whose mum had died and his retired father now too ill to care for him. His sisters, who had to travel, came at least once a month to take him out for the day and spoil him rotten.

The others rarely had visitors from family members and Diane's brother, who only lived a few miles away, didn't even bother to make the effort. The clients all had key staff members who managed their finances, took them shopping for clothes and so on when necessary, or to the doctor when required. Other good community-minded people took an interest in the clients' well-being and often took them for morning tea or outings for the day.

Holidays were also planned for them on a regular basis, generally using a small local business that specialised in organised holidays for the disadvantaged. The family issue was certainly a bone of contention, after all the clients couldn't help the way they had been born. As someone once said, "There but for the grace of God go I."

They drove into Blakesbrough and reached the trucking complex where Geoff stopped and indicated right to enter. While waiting for a couple of stock trucks to pass, he noticed a man standing in the yard. On seeing the distinctive van, he went quickly to the office door, said something and then scurried off, jumped into a car and disappeared rapidly.

A bit odd, he thought as he drove in and parked in the space marked "visitors".

"Come on, Diane," he said, handing her the chocolates. "You guys stay in the van, okay? We'll only be a few minutes and there's a bit of traffic going in and out."

"Okay Geoff, we will," said William. The rest just nodded or grunted in acquiescence.

Geoff and Diane entered the office and he asked the receptionist: "Is Larry about?"

"You've just missed him," she replied and wouldn't look him in the eye.

The penny dropped with Geoff. "That was him that took off when we arrived, wasn't it?" he asked.

"Um, yes," came the somewhat embarrassed reply.

He took the chocolates off Diane and brusquely thrust them at the girl. "Well, you tell him to have a very merry Christmas from Diane."

He turned disgustedly. "Come on, Diane, let's go. We know where we're not wanted."

"Gee, he pissed me off," Geoff said to Mandy later. "The bugger saw us coming and did a runner. That's really bloody great, you know. Poor Diane."

"About par for the course, unfortunately," said Mandy. "Generally they don't want to know. You just have to get used to it. Anyway, have a good weekend and we'll see you Monday."

"You too," said Geoff, shaking his head at the day's events.

He was lazing around at home on Sunday afternoon, having done the lawns and thinking about perhaps cracking open a beer when the phone rang. It was an over-excited Mandy screaming down the phone. "Geoff! Geoff! Have you checked the Lotto numbers?"

"Whoa, whoa," he replied. "You're blowing my eardrums. What was that?"

"Our Lotto numbers! Have you checked them?" she screamed

again. He got the gist of it this time. He'd actually forgotten all about it. His body suddenly tingled.

"No," he said almost breathlessly, "I left my copy hanging on the wall in the office. Have we won something?"

"YES! YES!" she screamed. "We've got six numbers and the Powerball! Six numbers! We've got the first division!"

"Bullshit! You're pulling my leg," he said. He gulped involuntarily. "We can't have ... can we?" The last almost whispered in a very small voice.

"No, we definitely have! Me and Bryan have checked and checked. We have! We've won!" The phone went quiet as this information began to sink in

"Are you there?" Mandy asked after some long seconds had elapsed.

"Yeah, I'm just trying to get my head around it. Are you sure? Have you checked on the internet?"

"We did and we're sure. Can you come round to the house about four? We're all going to meet and talk things over."

"I'll be there," he replied and after hanging up erupted in a loud "woo-oop woo-oop" like a monkey in the jungle. He danced madly and happily round the house

The actual amount won never even entered his mind at this stage, such was his euphoric state. He felt a sudden urge to tell someone and reached for the phone but then had sudden second thoughts. I haven't even seen the ticket yet. Better to make sure. Four o'clock. Four o'clock. He couldn't bloody wait.

The noise was cacophonic with everyone talking at once. Staff members, their partners and families, the clients standing there looking on, not understanding what the fuss was all about. Mary finally called for quiet.

"Okay," she said. "Well, congratulations everybody. There have been two winners, so it looks like we get to share $8.5 million between us. You know, I think that's approximately $850,000 each. It's absolutely unbelievable." There was a loud cheer.

"A problem I can foresee will be some issues with the clients' shares. Fortunately we handle their financial affairs within house, but I do suspect some of the families might well want to have something to say about that once they find out. I'll talk to management tomorrow but it will probably be best if we keep our win amongst ourselves, for the time being anyway. Is that okay with everybody?"

"Bugger the families," Geoff erupted. "Apart from Fred, they never come and visit anyway." There was a resounding chant of "hear hears" from the rest.

Mary agreed and continued: "If you have already told someone, try and get hold of them and ask them to keep it quiet if you can. I know it will be hard, because there will be so much conjecture, but I do think we need some time to sort things out before the win becomes public knowledge.

"All right now, let's organise! Who's going to go into Wellington tomorrow and register the ticket with the Lotto people? Probably ringing them first would be the best idea. Someone who's not on duty tomorrow, that is. Work goes on, you know."

There were a couple of disgruntled moans as just about every hand shot up to volunteer, and William immediately followed suit, causing a general laugh and a "good onya, William".

"Hey," someone suggested, "why not take him too? We can go on the train. He'd love that."

It was all organized and agreed, but the excited meeting continued for another hour before everyone began to happily drift away. Absolutely and totally unbelievable.

On the following Tuesday morning, the regional daily paper carried a story that someone in their little town had won a half share of the $17 million, which of course did cause much conjecture. It's hard to keep a secret, especially in a small town, so it was hardly a surprise when the midweek community newspaper said the winners were rumoured to be the staff and clients of a local CIL residence. It should really have been no surprise, then, when the following weekend the home was inundated with suddenly highly concerned and solicitous family members, who had suddenly somehow regained memory of their previously forgotten and ignored kin.

THE REFEREE

It was always the bloody same. Whenever their rugby club was on duty and had to provide referees for the kids' games at the city reserve, very few of the fathers turned up. There was a real scarcity of referees and most of the fathers certainly didn't want to be one, thank you very much. Actually it was probably no wonder, because really it was a thankless task.

Refs quite often found themselves the target of howls of abuse from mothers and fathers on the sideline, especially when their little Johnny's team wasn't doing so well. Parents from some of the bigger clubs seemed the worst, too. They just did not like seeing their kids' teams being beaten. Hell, one ref even got assaulted a few months ago. He gave the game away on the spot, leaving one fewer ref for them to rely on. But at least it hadn't been too bad this morning, so far anyway.

Brad had refereed three games on the trot, and there'd been very little controversy or even any abuse that he was aware of. Only one game to go now, he thought. Shit hot! I could do with a bit of a rest before my team plays. Thank God I'm not allowed to referee them.

The next game was an under-12 fixture between one of the big clubs, whose team was right at the top of the competition, and a much smaller country club from about 40km out of town. Like a lot of the smaller clubs, finance and transport were quite often a problem and sometimes their teams were short of players and had to call in younger ones who had already played, or even just default altogether.

It was a sad situation, really, but in general a lot of the small club players missed out on what the bigger clubs did for their own and certainly didn't get the opportunities they did. Brad had a look around. Ah, good. The country club seemed to have a full team, and a few parents present too. Excellent. He moved off to talk to the coaches before commence of play was signalled.

The game started and the first 10 minutes were hectic. There was a swag of parents from the big club on the sideline as usual, vociferously urging their kids on. But the country team, with a full complement of players the right age this time, were going well and got their noses slightly in front.

Did the opposition parents like it? Did they heck as like! The sledging had started even before the game, when a busybody parent had come over and complained that he thought some of the country team players were overage and overweight. Brad checked with the country team's coach, who had lists of the team and registered players. All seemed correct, and anyway the opposition seemed to have some bloody big boys in their team as well. Brad pointed this out to the complainant, who'd just sniffed and stalked off.

It was this dickhead who was now giving him the worst verbals: "You're bloody useless ref; that was a forward pass by a mile" "Knock on, you blind bastard" "You get that whistle out of a Weetbix packet?" "You're missing a good game you hopeless prick" and so on and so forth.

A few others were also giving him a bit of curry, mostly supporters of the big club. The country club people were just happy their team was in front, and urged their boys on for all their worth.

He penalized a big club player for a high tackle and the ignoramus spectator, the one doing most of the complaining, actually walked on to the field, apoplectic and spitting his abuse loudly for all to hear. The kick went over, giving the small club team an even bigger lead. Brad called halftime and talked to both teams and their coaches, telling them they were going well and to keep it up

He had a drink of water, then wandered over to the sideline and approached the abusive ignoramus. Holding up the whistle longways between his right index finger and thumb he said: "Hey mate, do you want to referee the second half?" The ignoramus obviously thought about starting up but noticed the ref's close and pugnacious stance, his red face, and hard-looking eyes. He thought better of it and just answered: "Um, no." "Good then," said the ref, "because if I hear one word of abuse from you in the second half, I'm going to shove this fuckin whistle right up your fuckin arse sideways." He stared hard at the man for a few seconds then asked: "You understand?" There was no reply. The ref repeated his question slowly, as if talking to a child, or an ignoramus. "Do you understand?" The man swallowed and just nodded his head. The second half was a cracker and the country team won, much to their delight. The ref's team also won much to his delight.

On the Monday evening, he received a call from his club's president saying that somebody had put in a complaint about his language during the game on Saturday.

"Fair go," he said to himself after hanging up. "I should have punched the bastard."

Then he called out to his wife: "Dear, do you think refs ever get sent off?"

A YOUNG FLAME

For my niece Justine – writer, poet, dancer, mother and a heap of other things – and her husband Andy, who encouraged, pushed and prodded me to get my stories into print.

Also for my moko, Adara, whose red hair was the inspiration for this story.

Somehow the guest list at his daughter's 9th birthday had grown from the agreed three to six.

It didn't really matter that much, though, because it was a simple enough menu to prepare: Barbecue chops and sausages, coleslaw and, as specified by the birthday girl, shop-bought chips.

There were also lollies, of course, and cupcakes, potato chips, a variety of soft drinks and an ice cream cake. All the usual and rather unhealthy suspects one would expect for a bunch of eight- or nine-year-olds.

The good part about it was that all Chris had to do was the barbecue, and his wife Annie made the cupcakes. The rest was pretty easily fixed, although they did have six noisy girls staying over for the night, which along with their six-year-old girl Kara plus the two boys, probably meant an extremely loud and late Saturday night.

Still, the kids could all watch movies and the girls were sleeping down in the games room, which was far enough away from their bedroom for the noise not to be too much of a problem.

Chris got the matches out of the top cupboard, grabbed a beer out of the fridge and went out to light the barbecue, which in his mind was always a good excuse to have a beer. While it was warming up, he came back in and threw the matches on top of the fridge, fully intending to put them back in the cupboard later. But he got sidetracked and ended up refereeing and running various games for the deliriously noisy girls, so it completely slipped his mind.

The party went off really well and after finally having got the over-excited girls settled and slowly drifting off to sleep one by one, Chris and Annie finally got to bed themselves sometime after 10pm.

"Dad! Dad!" An urgent voice filtered through the fog as Chris lay dozing, and he opened his eyes. It was his oldest boy Joe, a rising 11-year-old.

Forgetting what day it was, he instinctively looked at the clock radio. Shit, it was only 6.24 am. "What's up?" he asked rather grumpily.

"The bottom bunk's on fire, Dad," Joe said.

"What!" The fog suddenly vanished and, as he leapt out of the bed, he could suddenly smell smoke. Charging into the hall, he saw thick, black, toxic-looking smoke billowing out of the boys' room and spreading rapidly up the hall.

"Where's John?" he asked in a sudden panic as he raced down towards the bedroom, because John had slept in that bedroom too.

"In the games room watching TV, I think," came Joe's reply.

Heart pounding fiercely, and frightened for his kids and their guests, Chris raced past the smoking bedroom and did a quick headcount of the bodies down in the games room. Eight girls and one boy, all present and correct and unharmed. Thank God for that. He turned to Annie, who had also arrived on the scene by then and was standing next to Joe.

"Take them all out the sliding door into the back yard," he snapped, indicating the door from the games room, and then he turned and dived into the smoking bedroom, slamming the door shut behind him. The stench of the smoke was bloody awful and immediately got right up his nose, making him want to cough and his eyes water. So he held his breath and peered through the smoke at the bottom bunk.

The rubber mattress was well alight, blazing with a black liquid bubbling furiously in the middle. The flames were now licking strongly up the wall, not too far off setting that alight as well. Half gagging and with eyes watering in the thick hot, toxic atmosphere, he took the top end of the mattress and doubled it over in an endeavour to starve the flame of oxygen.

This had the immediate effect of shutting the flames down considerably, although the smoke seemed to worsen, so he raced to the far end of the bedroom and threw open the French doors leading out on to the balcony.

After sucking in a few quick breaths of sweet fresh air, which cleared his head somewhat, he returned to the still hideously spluttering and smoking mattress and, holding his breath gingerly, picked it up by both ends and hurried it out the French doors onto the balcony, throwing it down onto the back lawn.

He quickly darted back into the smoke-filled bedroom but no more flames were obvious, so he hurried back outside and, grabbing the backyard hose, turned the tap on.

Soon the mattress was hissing and spluttering as the water had the desired effect on the bubbling rubber. Having been entirely oblivious to anything else going on around him, he was surprised when he finally looked up to see all the kids giggling and pointing at him. Wondering what the hell that was all about, he looked down and suddenly saw! Shit! He was stark bollocky naked! Dropping the hose, he bolted back inside as fast as his legs could take him.

It took a while to get things sorted out but after making sure that there was no further fire inside the bedroom again and all the windows and doors in the house had been thrown open to air the place out, and everyone was decently fed (and clothed), they finally worked out what must have happened.

John, their youngest at nearly five and who slept in the bottom bunk, had woken up very early and going into the kitchen, must have seen the matches on top of the fridge. He had pushed a chair up next to the bench, climbed up and had just been able to reach them.

They surmised he returned to his room, put a blanket over his head started striking the matches. Fortunately he ran out of them and went down to the games room to watch TV with the girls, not even realizing that a blanket, sheet or quilt had been left smouldering.

It was just lucky Joe had woken up in time to raise the alarm and, more importantly, not to be burned.

Chris apologised to Annie. "It was my fault," he said. "I should have put the matches away straight away and not left them on top of the fridge."

"Well at least no one was injured, we are insured and maybe a lesson was learned," she replied gracefully. She knew Chris had had a hell of a big fright.

The rest of the day passed with no further excitement, although it was rather noticeable when the various parents came to pick up their girls later that afternoon, Chris kept a very low profile.

Later that night with the kids safely in bed – the boys, much to their delight, sleeping down in the games room because of the smoke damage to their room – Annie said: "You know, dear, you're really lucky you didn't get any of that burning rubber on you."

She snorted through barely contained laughter. "Because I don't think they do plastic surgery on dicks, do they?" With that she rolled onto her back on the bed, convulsing with great shudders of uncontrollable mirth. It didn't help matters too much when Chris started tickling her either.

Nine months later, almost to the day, an extremely healthy little girl exhibiting a fine set of lungs and flaming red hair was born. After some argument and discussion and given the unusual circumstances of her conception, it was eventually decided. They would call her Modesty Blaze.

It should have come as no shock when she soon began to exhibit a temperament in keeping with her hair, along with an outrageous sense of humour.

THE BOY

THE BOY

No amount of postulating or prostrating by the hierarchy is of any earthly use to the silent or fobbed-off victims.

The boy glanced fearfully yet again at the classroom clock. There was only just over a quarter of an hour to go until home time. The afternoon had flown by when he didn't want it to.

He swallowed nervously and stifled a yawn, not wanting to disturb old Ma Maggot, the boys' secret nickname for Sister Mary Margaret, whose voice droned on incessantly in the background. Her voice was as boring as ever; tone stuck at the same pitch, only ever varying when she caught someone not paying attention or fidgeting. Then it would rise suddenly to a querying crescendo, followed by a flash of black and the crash of a ruler.

You had to watch her all the time, the crabby old bitch. She was forever sneaking up behind you to see if you were doing what you were supposed to be doing.

If you weren't, you'd be the instant recipient of God's punishment – manifesting itself in the edge of a ruler fair across the knuckles.

Only if you were a boy, that was. Usually the girls didn't have to suffer that sort of atonement. If they happened to get caught, an uncommonly rare occurrence, it would usually be a telling-off or in the worst case, maybe a bit of an ear pull.

This year, in particular, he had noticed that a lot of the nuns, especially the elderly ones, didn't seem to like boys much at all. They were all very severe in dealing out punishment for real or imagined misdemeanours. If a girl committed the same crime, it did not have the same heinous implications, in their holy minds.

There was only one boy in the class whose name very rarely

seemed to feature on the list of sinners. Perhaps the fact that his father was a very successful local businessman, was on the council, and often made lucrative, well-publicised donations to the church could well have something to do with it.

All in all, it was a worry at times, getting punished for something you were supposed to have done but sometimes not even knowing what it actually was. Like one day, when he'd only just arrived at school, he was sent for and told he'd broken a window earlier that morning and would have to pay for it. Of course, he protested his innocence vehemently, even going as far to say he could actually prove he wasn't even there at the time.

The trouble was that his accuser was one of the nuns. And if you did have the utter temerity to call into question the word of a nun, a representative of God on earth who in no way could ever be wrong, well. That was regarded as an even bigger sin than the original one in their eyes, making you doubly dammed.

Old Ma Maggot was known as one of the worst of the boy-haters in the school, too. She had this way of asking the boys difficult questions that she knew they wouldn't know the answer to. As the question was being asked, invariably something to do with religion, each boy in the class bar one would slump lower and lower in his desk, trying hard not to be noticed. But it was always just a waste of time. Old Maggot always knew exactly who she was going to ask next.

As each nominated boy stood and failed to give the right answer, he was berated for his stupidity and told to remain standing while Maggot delightedly reminded the girls it just proved her oft-repeated theory that boys had lower intelligence than them.

She'd then move on to her next victim, and would never be satisfied until there were at least seven or eight boys standing. After further expanding on her favourite theory of male un-intelligence, she'd usually say: "Come on then girls, let's tell the boys the answer."

If no female hands went up, as was quite often the case, Maggot would mouth the words slowly, exaggerating the vowels so the girls could easily follow and mumble them slightly after her. Then after a "well done girls", the stupid boys would be told to sit down while Maggot and the girls always had another good laugh at their humiliation.

"Boy? Boy?" A querulous voice broke into his reverie. Oh no, she'd copped him not listening. "You're not paying attention, are you? What did I just say"?

The boy knew there was no use trying to lie, he was well and truly caught, "I don't know, sister," he said.

"Stand up!" snapped the nun. "You can remain behind after the others have gone, and I'll give you something to do that might remind you to pay attention while I'm speaking."

"I can't stay back tonight, sister," the boy started to explain. But she broke in.

"Oh, that's right," she said. "I'd forgotten about that. You have to report to the presbytery, don't you? It won't surprise me at all if you're in trouble there as well. You can stay back tomorrow after school, then. And remain standing till home time. That might help you keep your mind where it should be."

She turned back to the class and starting winding up the day's lessons.

The boy took her punishment stoically. He was well used to it. Maggot had her favourite list of sinners to pick on, and if his name was not on top, it surely mustn't be too far off it.

Mind you, part of it was probably his fault. Earlier that year, when they were having a few words, she'd told him that he was as bold as brass, and on the way home in the bus that night, he had reported this fact to one of the older boys. The boy cheekily suggested next time she said that, he should ask her how bold brass was.

The occasion had arisen sooner than expected, so he had asked the question, outraged the Maggot and duly found him paraded in front of the head nun. He was accused of heinous crime of insubordination to one of God's representatives on earth, along with a whole pile of other venial sins that he couldn't actually remember committing. Old Maggot certainly wasn't above embellishing any wrong-doings to make them seem even worse.

He was strapped, and then severely threatened with even more dire consequences if he should listen to the devil again. His at-best tenuous relationship with Old Maggot had taken a definite turn for the worse.

But she was the least of his worries at the moment. An incident several months ago had shocked him to the very core. It had been an unfathomable event. Worse, it was still being repeated, plunging the boy into a nightmarish dilemma.

With sinking heart, he heard the bell go, and Maggot finally dismissed the class. Woodenly, he began to gather his books together, the noise of happy home-going chatter and banging of desk-tops somehow mocking his own desperate plight.

He walked numbly up the driveway to the school gate, his legs somehow forcing an unwilling body onwards. He was so oblivious to the excited chatter of the other kids filing eagerly out that he didn't even notice a couple of his friends try and talk to him. His mind was instead totally fixated on where he was going and what had happened there previously.

He crossed the road when the monitors lifted their poles, totally unaware of the crush of the other kids about him, then turned and walked towards the large, 100-year-old stone church, a place that was once welcoming but now definitely sinister.

Even with his eyes cast downwards, somehow the steeple still loomed dark and ominous in his peripheral vision. Another boy yelled his name, but he was so caught up in his own misery and dread that he didn't even notice.

Up the drive to the church, then turn on to the presbytery path on the right, passing old-fashioned headstones from which he and a couple of mates had once secretly prised lead lettering to sell as scrap.

The legs somehow kept forcing the oh-so-reluctant body onwards.

The tall, dark, old-fashioned, two-storey building loomed up as he drew closer. He desperately wanted to turn and bolt, but knew it would do no good in the end.   He felt suddenly sick and had to clench his buttocks as his bowels loosened and threatened to explode.

In desperation, he looked around for something that might save him – anything, anything at all. Someone else arriving, perhaps, or a strange car parked outside signalling a visitor's presence, another priest on the balcony, anything that might offer some distraction.

But he was clutching at straws. There was nothing. No distraction, no salvation today.

The boy shivered in apprehension, even though it was a warm day, then slowly and unwillingly forced himself round the side of the sombre old building and knocked timidly on the big solid wooden back door.

"You've come to see the Father, then," the warm-hearted, middle-aged Irish housekeeper greeted him upon opening the door. She had a broad accent and a great sense of humour and in earlier, much happier times not so long ago, he had always enjoyed listening to and trying to understand her talk in a delightful Gaelic lilt. But in his present state of utter despair, he didn't even notice it. He just nodded dumbly.

Puzzled by his serious and downcast demeanour, she said: "He's in his rooms. You know where they are." He nodded dumbly again and entered, robotically as though in a trance.

The housekeeper watched him enter and scratched her head

perplexedly. "A few months ago I would have sworn that boy had kissed the Blarney Stone," she said to herself. "But now look at him; he must be in trouble. Oh well, perhaps the good Father can help him out."

She quickly put it out of her mind and went about her duties. never realising the boy had been mutely begging her for help with desperate eyes, and had regarded her as his last chance.

"Come in," the voice said almost immediately after he had knocked very timidly.

He opened and entered the large cold room, and stood stock still just inside the doorway gazing fearfully at the short, solid bespectacled figure dressed in black seated at the desk.

"Close the door and come over here," the figure commanded.

As he obeyed, the figure rose, walked around the desk and clumped heavily over to the door and turned the key. The solid thunking of the old-fashioned lock evaporated the boy's last hope of any salvation.

"Sit here, boy," the dark figure commanded, indicating a large antique leather sofa against the wall. The boy obeyed, positioning himself as far away as possible from the priest, who had now reseated himself behind the desk.

"You know why I've sent for you, don't you?" the priest asked after staring unblinkingly at him for some 20 seconds or so.

The boy remained quiet, his huge frightened eyes staring back at the priest.

"Well, I'm waiting," the priest said, after more seconds of bewildered silence from the boy.

A "no Father" finally rasped from an ever so dry throat.

"Have you got anything to confess to me?" the priest asked.

The boy swallowed with difficulty and started: "Well, I got into trouble at school today and ..."

"I don't mean today, boy," the priest broke in irately. "What did you do last weekend?"

"Nothing, Father," the boy answered.

"What do you mean, nothing? You know where you go if you tell lies, don't you?" There was a short silence. Then, in a louder voice: "Now, tell me the truth! What did you do last weekend?"

"I, I played footy on Saturday and went to church on Sunday, Father," the boy replied, full knowing that this was not what the priest wanted to hear.

Silence for long seconds while the priest stared at him unblinkingly again, then came a curt: "Nothing else?"

"No, Father."

The priest stared angrily at him for what seemed like an age, then said: "Well, I've had a report about you and another boy from the weekend, and I've since spoken to him. He told me what you two got up to. I must say I'm disappointed in you after our last little chat. It seems as though you've deliberately set out to disobey me. Now, do you want to tell me what you got up to?"

"Nothing, Father," came the quavering reply. The boy was on the verge of tears. He knew that something awful was going to occur now.

The priest rose to his feet head, shaking in frustration. "You still deny your sins, even though I have the proof?"

Clumping noisily over to the door he then turned around, "I have to make a couple of phone calls and then I'll have a cup of tea. I'll leave you to reflect on things until I get back."

There was another short pause before the priest spoke again to his helpless, quaking victim. "Do you want me to have to ring your parents and tell them what you've been up to? Just think about how upset they'd be, and then what would happen if the nuns and the whole school found out as well? What would that do to your family's name? Your poor mother would be mortified. Think about it when I'm gone, boy, think about it well."

The door closed, the heavy thunk leaving an abjectly fearful boy miserable and uncomprehending. He simply had no idea what it was he was supposed to have done. He didn't even know who the other boy was, although he was well used to that sort of scenario from the nuns.

But he was frightened now. Desperately frightened of what the priest might require him to do to earn forgiveness. Half-vomiting, he hurriedly swallowed the bile and, such was his fear, he felt the need to go to the toilet again. Being locked into the room, he was even denied that relief.

He settled down to wait ever more nervously for the return of his tormentor, who now had him in his complete power.

ϕ—ϕ

The nightmare had begun some two months previously. The priest had got into the habit of dropping off typing at his home for his mother to do for the church. As it was the school holidays, on this occasion he'd asked if the boy could come and help him redecorate his elderly aunt's place while she was away.

The boy hadn't wanted to go because he hadn't liked the way the priest had rubbed his hand up and down his thigh on a previous occasion when he had got him alone in his car. But they hadn't even asked him if he wanted to go and his mother, seemingly in awe of the attention of the holy man, had accepted eagerly on his behalf. He had no option.

Things had been all right for a while. Although he had found stripping the wallpaper repetitious and boring, he persisted with it and after a few hours they had stopped for a break. Finding a soft drink in the fridge, he'd sat on the sofa with it and then had been quite bewildered when the priest had come and sat right next to him. The priest's thigh was touching his and then he began rubbing his hand up and down all over the boy's thighs and lower body.

The boy tried to move away, but the priest had just crushed his body tighter against him, using his outstretched legs to hem him in. Soon the priest, who seemed somehow strangely aroused and was breathing funnily, stopped and asked if he had liked it.

On a negative reply, the priest suggested that perhaps this was because he still had his clothes on, and it would be a lot more enjoyable if he removed them. The boy, in a state of utter confusion at these goings-on, refused. The now extraordinarily stimulated priest curtly ordered his young charge to strip, and then began hurriedly stripping him anyway.

He then forced the boy to lie on his back on the sofa while he massaged him all over, concentrating particularly around the genital area.

Eventually dropping all pretence of not focusing on the boy's genitals, he then began fondling and stroking them, panting heavily and a fixed flushed stare on his face. Then to add to the boy's complete and utter confusion and consternation, he confounded him even further when he knelt and began kissing and sucking them.

Not understanding these terrible events at all and at a complete loss as to what to do, the boy began sobbing quietly to himself and turned his head toward the back of the sofa in a futile attempt to block out what was occurring. The priest carried on like this for what seemed like forever but was probably only no longer than five or six minutes.

Stopping momentarily, the priest hurriedly took off his own pants, then started again, sucking and moaning, one hand active below the sofa out of the boy's sight doing something to himself as well.

The boy didn't know what to think. It was way beyond his juvenile comprehension. He just lay there, naked, helpless, in a totally troubled and confused state of mind. Eventually the priest gave a loud moan and the boy felt something warm and sticky splattering all over his stomach, legs and chest. The priest collapsed on top of him and gave him a kiss, which he was not quite quick enough to avoid receiving on the lips.

The boy was pinned and couldn't move while the priest lay there inert but breathing heavily, the acrid smell of cigarettes on his breath. Eventually, he did move, pulling up his pants and ordering the boy brusquely to go to the bathroom, clean himself up and put his clothes back on.

The boy moved quickly, needing no second invitation to get out of there. He disappeared eagerly, locked himself in the toilet and tried vainly to comprehend what had just occurred. Nothing he'd ever learned in his short life so far could explain it.

After some 20 minutes or so of cowering in the false sanctuary of the toilet, he was ordered out by the priest, who said it was time to go home. They packed up and left.

The boy was quiet all the way, as if in shock, while the priest began rubbing his thigh again and saying that it was the privilege of God's love he had given him, and it would be better if he told nobody else. He said that his sins and the penance he had to do were only to be kept between the two of them and God. Nobody else would believe him if he told them anyway.

The boy said nothing because he was sorely troubled, in fact absolutely stunned, as the priest dropped him off at home without another word, not even bothering to go inside. There was not much sleep to be had that night nor the following nights, months and years. The boy's innocence and childhood had been forever shattered.

His mother noticed that he was uncommonly quiet over the next few days and asked if he was feeling ill. He said no, but that's all he could say. He had no words that could ever explain what had happened to him. How could he? How could he talk about something that was way beyond his tender juvenile comprehension? Or how he had been betrayed by one of the very people into whose hands his mother had entrusted his spiritual education?

At school he began running into far more trouble than usual, his moods ranging from dumb insolence right to the other end of the scale as he became a totally disruptive and comical influence. He began to loathe school, wagging some days, late on others, never doing his homework, and always, always ever so afraid he'd see the priest or be sent for.

After successfully avoiding him for more than two weeks, his worst fears were confirmed when he was ordered to report to the presbytery again after school.

More of the same had occurred on that occasion, although the priest was a lot quieter this time in his own locked rooms, almost as if he didn't want to be overheard. He'd also turned the boy over onto his stomach on the sofa this time, rubbing his penis between the cheeks of the bewildered boy's buttocks until the same sticky warm substance had splattered all over his back and buttocks.

After another curt "get dressed", and a reminder that it was God's will, he was sent on his way. When the poor, bewildered boy finally arrived at home, who was sitting in the lounge with his mother, smiling angelically with a cup of tea in his hand? No one else but the cunning, deviant priest.

The boy was devastated. There was nowhere he could feel safe, not even in the supposed sanctuary his own home. Feeling disgust and loathing for both himself and the priest, he ran the bath, locked the door and lay in the hot water for a long, long time, scrubbing his back and buttocks as best he could as if somehow trying to wipe away the awful stain.

When the priest finally left, his mother knocked on the bathroom door and berated him loudly for ignoring the presence of the holy man. The boy took the criticism silently. He could say nothing, he didn't know how to.

He'd managed to successfully avoid the priest for the following month or so after this incident, due to the fact that right out of the blue he had developed asthma, in spite of nobody else in the family ever having had it. He thankfully missed many days of school, blessing the ailment because it denied the priest the chance to prey on him.

The asthma was a real puzzle to his mother and the family doctor, who said there didn't seem to be any clinical reason for it, so it must be an allergy or nervous reaction to something.

The boy couldn't find the words to say anything, how could he? And of course he wouldn't be believed anyway – something the cunning deviant priest had always counted on.

The boy waited quietly, fearfully. He was busting for a crap and needed to pee something chronic, the dread of what might occur making his nerves work overtime. The priest had been gone for a long time now he wanted to go home, he wanted his mother, he …

The lock clunked suddenly and the solid, black-clad, bespectacled figure framed the doorway. "Well boy, have you decided to confess?"

The figure momentarily paused, the lock clunked again. When the priest finally moved towards him, his frightened eyes noticed that the key had gone from out of the lock. No hope now, no hope at all.

The priest seated himself behind the desk again. "Come and stand here, boy," he said indicating a spot directly in front of him. "Now, what have you got to say for yourself?"

The boy remained silent, frightened into muteness.

"So, you won't confess?"

"I don't know what it is I'm supposed to have done, Father," the boy finally rasped out of a dry, so very dry, throat. It was almost a whisper.

"So, you still deny it then? You know God loves you and has the power to forgive you, don't you?"

"Yes Father." The whisper again.

"You know God gives me the power to love and forgive you on his behalf?"

The boy could only mouth the "yes Father" this time.

"Take your clothes off." A direct order. The boy stood, stunned, motionless.

"Take your clothes off," a more steely tone. The priest watched until the boy stood a slender body quivering in its underpants. "All of them."

The boy slowly slid his underpants off.

"Come around here."

The boy obeyed and the priest, the holy man of God, swivelled his chair, pulled the boy between his legs, back towards him then began fondling his genitals and kissing the back of his neck.

The boy sobbing quietly and abandoned all hope trying to switch his mind off the terrible invasion of his body that followed.

The Mother

She was at her wits' end. Over the past six months, her son had gone from being a bright breezy and cheeky but likable child to being a sullen morose and totally uncommunicative one, especially at home. He could also veer right to the other end of the scale, becoming a virtually uncontrollable and completely disruptive influence at school.

He was showing no interest at all in his schoolwork, which had gone totally to pot. Most of the time he didn't even bother with homework, generally saying he didn't have any. His mother had tackled him many times about his behaviour but mostly he wouldn't even talk to her. This was a dreadfully hurtful thing from her favourite child.

He was arriving home later and later in the afternoons, and had been late for school on many occasions. Sometimes he never even got there, she had discovered when the complaints started coming in. Detentions didn't work, groundings didn't work and when she had reluctantly agreed to let her husband give him a thrashing, even that didn't work.

It was like water off a duck's back. His behaviour became worse and so did his asthma, causing him to miss yet even more schooling.

The mother had even gone as far as speaking with the head nun, suggesting that perhaps there might be a clash of personalities between the boy and Sister Mary Margaret. That had been a rather unfortunate suggestion, because the head nun had taken it as criticism of the nuns and had got rather angry.

The head nun said that God had called them to be teachers, educators of the young. Was she saying that God could be wrong? This intimidated the mother, coming as it did from the rather severe and aloof head nun, so she didn't bother to pursue that avenue any further.

The head did agree that the boy was a definite problem child though and would bear close watching if his present behaviour continued. The unfortunate spin-off from this was that the head took it upon herself to keep a closer watch on him and attempted to exorcise the devil out of him with liberal lashings of the strap.

This failed miserably, and when asked why he continually caused trouble, the boy would say nothing.

What really hurt the mother further was when the police brought him home – twice now it had happened, once for shoplifting from Woolworths and once for stealing bottles from the back of a dairy and taking them round the front to cash them in again.

The head nun hadn't helped matters by calling him out in front of the morning assembly after the shoplifting offence and using his public humiliation and punishment as a deterrent to others.

The mother had been devastated at that incident but hadn't complained because there had been some talk of expelling him from the school if his conduct didn't improve.

The priest had tried to help too, by offering to take him away to a weekend camp, "to try and talk some sense to him", he'd said. But the boy had developed asthma and had had to miss it.

So yes, she was at her wits' end and just didn't know what to do. Some said it was just a phase they go through, but the older children hadn't been as bad as him. They hadn't even been half as bad. A psychiatrist had been one suggestion and she had given it some serious thought. But there was no way of telling if he would speak to one anyway. Some days, he just wouldn't say a word.

A single tear slid down her cheek. What was to become of her youngest child? Wiping her cheek with an abstract backhand she stood suddenly, deciding to check on him in his room.

She opened the door slowly and let in enough light from the hall so she could see.

He was lying asleep on his back, bare-chested and uncovered from the waist up. The window directly behind the bed was wide open with the breeze blowing in and sitting right in the middle of his chest purring madly was Rosy the family cat.

The mother quickly shooed the cat out the window, closed the window then covered the boy up. It was as if he didn't even care about anything anymore. He had been told and told about leaving the window open at night, especially with his asthma. He didn't even seem to care whether he lived or died.

"What's wrong? What's wrong, son," the mother begged mutely as another tear appeared and slid down her cheek, a tiny pearl of mother's love. About to leave, she stooped and kissed him, shaking her head in despair. Deep down, she was certain he wasn't a bad boy. Why was he like this? What had they done wrong? Another tear slid down her cheek as she left the room, quietly closing the door.

The poor mother was not to get much sleep that night, worried as she was. Nor was she going to get any answers in the rest of her lifetime. The answers would only begin to come nearly half a lifetime later. Late, almost too late, for one already shattered and ruined young life.

The boy was eight years old.

MORE BMS BOOKS

Enjoyed this book? The following list of books is available from BMS Books.

A Soldier's Life by Lou Geraets

My Life…the Meanderings of Pop Knill by Lou Geraets

The Last Newspaper in the World by Mick Stone

Autumn and Other Stories by Rotorua Writers Group

The Forgotten by Sarah Groot

Forestry, People and Places – Selected Writings from Five Decades by Dennis Richardson

Demons Inside My Mind – Life with Anorexia – Jenna Oldham

LOCAL BOOKS

Local Books is a service provided by BMS to help self-published writers and other independent publishers to market their books. The services helps provide a new way into sometimes hard to access markets.

For more information about BMS Books and Local Books, contact:
BMS Books
5 High Street, Glenholme
Rotorua 3010
New Zealand
Email: ms@bms.co.nz
URL: www.bms.co.nz
Tel: 64-7-349 4107